A Business of Ferrets

Alwyn Bathan

Stairwell Books //

Published by Stairwell Books
161 Lowther Street
York, YO31 7LZ

www.stairwellbooks.co.uk
@stairwellbooks

ISBN: 978-1-913432-23-2

Cover design Alan Gillott with Sydney Luntz and Caitlin Brown
Imagery: Amira Talha, Wectors
Layout design: Alan Gillott
P5

To every child I've had the privilege of teaching in my thirty-nine years' service – thank you

Table of Contents

Chapter One – An Escaped Shoe

'A PERFECTLY GOOD EXPLANATION WHY your shoe went over the fence, Hilton?' his dad asked. 'Go on, then. Explain.'

Hilton had been showing off at the time. His dad had the fed-up sound that always followed a phone call from school.

All Hilton had wanted to do was impress Alanah, but she only liked football and he only liked the natural world.

He had decided to take a long kick towards goal and didn't worry one jot that his lace had worked its way loose. His shoe took flight like a hungry sparrowhawk *(A Walk in the Wild- A Field Guide, sparrowhawk, scientific name- Accipiter nisus, page 7)* across the sky. When it headed towards the high metal fence with the spikey top that no-one was allowed to climb, Hilton knew he was in trouble.

Each time his dad spoke to him, the latest 'incident' was added to the long list of Hilton's previous wrong doings.

'So, you're going to tell me, Hilton, you-

accidentally sent your shoe over the fence, like you -

accidentally put your half-eaten apple in the boys' urinal because it needed a plug. Was it like that? Or perhaps, it was more like the time you -

accidentally broke Imran's unbreakable ruler, or... when you – *accidentally* upset Alanah by showing her the squirrel with a broken arm?'

His dad looked hacked off, Hilton thought. It was nothing to do with today.

'I fixed that squirrel, (it was grey, *Sciurus carolinensis, page 4*) and Alanah was impressed,' he said, his shoulders rising a little. 'Bit of flour and water then toilet paper. Wait for it to set. Hard as plaster of Paris.' He knocked on the table to demonstrate.

Apart from Hilton trying to score the best overhead kick in history, he knew the real reason his dad was miffed.

He was a loser. His mum told him so whenever she thought Hilton couldn't hear.

When his dad left the laptop to get a cuppa, Hilton could see he'd been playing games. Hilton would wander past the screen, and BETWELL would be there in big green letters, and occasionally, messages like, 'YOU HAVE WON £14.' But, most often, the screen would say, 'SORRY, LOST THIS TIME. TRY AGAIN!' in red letters.

Usually, it was a horse racing game or playing cards. And his dad won, sometimes. But his mum said, 'sometimes' wasn't often enough.

Chapter Two – Packed Off with the Weasels

OVER TEA THAT NIGHT, HILTON'S mum cleared her throat.

Earlier, she and dad had been in a quiet huddle which was never a good sign. But, as she did that wrinkly-nose-thing she wasn't aware of, Hilton checked the detail from his best ever book, *A Walk in the Wild- A Field Guide*.

Their discussion had continued like a hare-boxing match, she, stepping forward to make sure Dad listened, he, backing away until there was nowhere to go.

Hilton flicked to the correct page. Yes, he thought. Definitely.

Brown hare, Lepus euripaeus, page 29. Tall and lean (both of them), *the brown hare has longer ears than its cousin, the rabbit.* (She can hear him on his mobile from downstairs.) *They have excellent vision* (she constantly looks over his shoulder at his computer screen) *and, mainly nocturnal, they forage at night* ('Joe!' she shouts, 'You've got that fridge door open again!'). *Whilst it's commonly believed the act of 'boxing' is carried out by male hares during Spring months, this is actually the female of the species, warning off the male.* ('I'm right, Joe. Bop, bop, biff. Take that!')

Mum's 'Worries from School' chat started in the usual way.

'You're ten, Hilton. Everything in life isn't about you.' Hilton knew her script off by heart. '*You've got to start thinking of others,*' would come next.

She had her back to him and a cloth in her hand, pretending to wipe the cooker surface but the hob was already sparkling. Cleaning always happened when there were tough things to be said.

'So, your dad and I have been talking, and we think you should spend some time over the summer with Uncle Norbert... Remember him? Lend a hand with his ....erm....oh...what are they called?' she tutted, looking across at his dad who was flicking the screen of his mobile. 'Weasels, are they?'

Hilton laughed, but his mum kept wiping, her hand going over and over in the same circles with a bright yellow cloth.

'They're ferrets, Mum,' he corrected. 'Weasels *(Mustela nivalis, page 13)* are wild. Ferrets *(Mustela putorius furo, page 18,* so different, can't you hear?) are tame.'

'Norbert's ferrets have *never* been tame. They bit you, after all.'

'A good reason to send me back for more,' Hilton sniffed.

'You're great with animals,' his mum went on. 'Everyone at school said so after you mended the squirrel's broken arm-paw-thing. I'll ring Norbert tonight, see what he thinks.'

HILTON WAS MEANT TO BE tucked up in bed with *A Walk in the Wild-A Field Guide,* but he was listening to everything downstairs. The living room door had been left open.

Although Hilton's eyes were, technically, looking at the page, the words were not fluttering off like red admirals *(Vanessa atalanta, page 33)* as usual, and landing inside the nature department of his brain. He was too busy concentrating on the row.

'If *you'd* stop wasting money on gambling, we could afford a holiday, Joe,' his mum said.

No matter how hard he strained his pipistrelle bat-ears *(Pipistrellus pipistrellus, page 45,* what a name, what a joke!) Hilton couldn't hear his dad's reply, but the conversation soon came back round to him.

'Hilton's behaviour has nothing to do with my games,' his dad said, 'but, if you want a summer holiday, *you* could do more cleaning shifts, Donna.'

His mum exhaled loudly by way of a reply. Sometimes, she required no words at all. 'Hilton needs sorting. If he's at Norbert's, he won't be getting into trouble during the school holiday.'

Then, someone closed the living room door.

Hilton reluctantly slid out of his warm nocturnal habitat, pulling over the woodland animals duvet cover to keep in the heat. He crept silently, remembering to avoid the creaky floorboard, to the top of the stairs where he could hear his mum on the phone.

'Norbert? You took a long time to answer…ah, I keep forgetting you've no mobile…how's things with you and your skunks? No, no, just kidding,' she said, 'I know, I know, they're ferrets.'

Skunks? Must double-check skunks.

HILTON RE-JOINED HIS WOODLAND friends when the deed was done. He pulled the red squirrel print close to his face. He might see an actual one, out there at Uncle Norbert's. But he could guarantee seeing lots of those wiggly things with fast feet and flashing fur.

And teeth.

Very sharp ones.

Lots of them.

Chapter Three – The East Northumbria Ferret Boarding and Welfare Society

HILTON'S HEART BEAT EXTRA HARD. Something inside his head was whooshing very loud.

He'd not seen Uncle Norbert since starting primary school and could vividly remember meeting a ferret for the first time. He'd been so excited to handle the little creatures, long and woolly like over-stretched rats. He'd gazed at the row of cages inside Norbert's shed. Behind each wire mesh were a couple of mini panda faces and bodies like furry bendy busses.

When Norbert took out Rodney, the smallest male with his bandit-mask face, Hilton had loved the way the tiny feet and claws dug into his palms. This cute, furry being scrabbled and dodged across his hand. When it stopped for a moment, Hilton could feel its heart, beating a whole lot faster than his.

PUMP-PUMP-SLOSH-SLOSH-BOOM-BOOM, it went.

'Whoa! That's mint!' he'd shouted. A little too loudly, perhaps. But he was only four. The creature bit his middle finger and hung by its sharp, white teeth for what seemed like hours.

Hilton had given the little chap a huge shock, Uncle Norbert said. Rodney hadn't chomped into anyone before.

But Rodney hung there…

like washing…

on the line…

his teeth as pegs.

Hilton could still feel that pain today. He had been too afraid to look Rodney in the eye in case he became more cross, and bit even harder. Hilton could not shake him off.

The waggling ferret suspended there...like a pendulum. Well, it was too much for a four-year-old.

Uncle Norbert had laughed out loud as he tapped Rodney on the snout, once, very gently. 'Let go,' he said, pushing his forefinger between its jaws which opened automatically like lift doors.

The ferret bite cut their visit short that day. His mum had insisted they go home via the hospital, for that special injection, the one that wouldn't hurt at all, to stop the wound turning nasty.

After that, Hilton had cried whenever his parents mentioned going to Uncle Norbert's again.

AFTER HIS PAINFUL INTRODUCTION TO ferret-handling, Hilton was more than a little anxious as his dad drove slowly up the bumpy dirt track just wide enough for their car, and nothing else. As they turned, there was a sign leaning to one side, with brown writing and hand-painted pictures of ferrets. The portraits of the animals were incomplete- missing ears and feet mainly, where the paint had cracked and peeled, and some letters were missing from the words.

EA T NO THUMB A FERRET BOA IN   AND ELF SOC TY, it read.

'What's that meant to say?' Hilton asked, glad to find something, anything, to think about other than his pounding heart.

'East Northumbria Ferret Boarding and Welfare Society,' his mum said. 'Always had grand ideas, your Uncle Norbert. Shame it's come to nothing.'

'I get the East Northumbria bit,' Hilton said. 'But, Boarding and Welfare Society?'

'Norbert'll explain,' his dad shrugged. 'They're all Greek to me, ferrets. Or are they Polish? I can never remember.' *(The domestic ferret is thought to be a domesticated Western or Eastern European polecat, page 18.)*

They came to a halt outside a house as ramshackle as the sign at the end of the lane. Hilton's dad tooted the horn. 'Don't get out yet,' he said. 'Looks like a bomb's dropped since we were here last.'

The porch had several bricks missing and tiles had slid gracefully down the roof to form an overhanging edge, a bit like a ski slope which finished in the gutter. It looked ready to lurch over and land in the garden with a clatter like drunken old men, probably bringing the roof down too, Hilton thought.

Uncle Norbert appeared in the doorway with a huge smile. A large man with a rounded middle and greying hair, he wore brown cord trousers, a paler shade at the knees where they were bald from repeated kneeling. His large green knitted jumper had strands escaping like overcooked spaghetti, one of which caught on a nail sticking out from the doorframe as he walked towards the car. He pushed up a pair of glasses from his dripping nose to view the boy more clearly.

'Ah, my apprentice!' he said, his arms outstretched, his jumper unravelling with each step. Like a dog on a short lead, he twanged to a halt and tugged at the wool pulling him back towards house. 'Needs a hammer. Hilton, that's your first job.'

His mum swallowed hard. She looked at her son. They were thinking the same thing, he imagined. Hilton wasn't ready for a hammer.

'*Remind me to fix the door,*' Uncle Norbert said. Hilton and his mum sighed together in relief. 'Now lad, get your bag out of the boot. I'll take you round the back to meet the lads and lasses.'

'You've got other helpers, Uncle?' Hilton asked.

'The *ferrets*, boy! They are *my* lads and lasses.' He banged his big claw-like hand on the car boot so Hilton's dad would open it. 'Come see my empire, Joe, Donna. It's grown a bit since you were here last.'

A smell of something unmentionable wafted towards the boy.

The native badger, Meles meles, page 13. The boar, or dominant male, leads a solitary existence. (Was there an Aunt when I was here last?) *Thick set, rounded and powerful* (true*), the badger has poor eyesight* (not helped by tape holding his glasses together), *and emits an unpleasant scent from a gland at the base of his tail* (confirmed) *when alarmed or, during mating* (URGH, LET ME SKIP IMMEDIATELY TO THE NEXT PAGE).

Uncle Norbert charged ahead to the back of the house, thrilled to be showing off his life's work, as Hilton's dad followed carrying his bag.

The sight that greeted them took their breath away.

Chapter Four – The Re-appearance of Rodney

HIDDEN FROM VIEW BEHIND THE house and stretching as far Hilton's eyes could see, were sheds.

Each one made from different materials.

All joined together.

Some were created from fence panels. Others had lived on allotments, been removed and rebuilt in the most higgledy-piggledy way. There was a shed made from a double decker bus and one from an old camper van. They were laid out in rows and probably meant to be straight, but because each building was constructed from something different, they didn't fit together at all. The streets were wonky and looked tipsy. They wound their way over what had been a lush lawn last time Hilton was there. Now, there was no grass and no garden, just sheds. Wobbly, mismatched, propped against one another like old pals waiting for the bingo to open on a Friday night.

'*This* is where my lads and lasses live,' Uncle Norbert said, proudly, waving his arm across the buildings he'd spent so much time and effort constructing.

Hilton watched his mum's face. She had a smile at first, but as her eyes continued to take in every roof, every door and window of the view, her mouth fell open.

His dad nudged her ribs gently, so Uncle Norbert didn't see. 'Very proud of his establishment, your brother,' he whispered from the corner of his mouth. 'Maybe *we* should do the same in *our* back garden?'

As his mum and dad left, Hilton could hear them bicker all the way back to the car and even down the lane, about whether they should actually be leaving him there. (*The spring hare-boxing continues through to summer, page 29.*)

Uncle Norbert didn't seem to notice. He was too busy showing Hilton how he'd spent the time since his last visit.

His uncle had a name for every shed. They went into the first one ('Bluebell Lodge,' he said), with cages and runs and pens and enclosures. These were all made in the same disorderly, tottering way as the buildings, cobbled together from this and that, left overs and offcuts, whatever Norbert had found over the years, dumped in the lanes and offered by people demolishing theirs to buy bigger, posher versions.

'*This* is where the magic happens,' the old man said. 'Inside here are all my prize-worthy animals.' He pulled at a rickety creaking door which flexed and shuddered as he moved it.

'Don't you need locks on the doors to keep them safe, the winners?' Hilton asked, looking a bit confused.

'You're not *listening* properly, son,' his uncle replied. 'They're *worthy* of prizes, but they never win nowadays. Anyway, let's meet the best boy, Rodney,' he said, pursing his lips and squinting to find the right creature. Hilton felt his heart leap.

'Rodders, Rodders, where are you?' he said, in a gentle, sing-songy way, followed by a few puffs of a whistley noise that resembled no tune at all.

The ferret-washing hanging from his finger was all the boy could think about. He remembered Rodney who had nipped him so viciously that day when he was just four. He rubbed his middle finger against his thumb, feeling the pain again and imagining those sharp little teeth clinging on so determinedly.

'I don't think...I don't...want....' Hilton started.

'No, lad, this is grandson of Rodney....Rodders the third,' his uncle said, picking up this furry critter then that, turning them over, tutting and putting them down when they weren't the one he was looking for.

Then, there was a squeak.

A ferret, one brown eye and one red, skipped into the old man's hand. He smiled and stroked it playfully, feeding the bendy body through his right hand, then the left, and back again. He kept it going, knitting its length between his hands, until its figure-of-eights made Hilton feel dizzy.

'After you were bitten by Rodney the first, I changed their food *and* the way I handled them, especially for the competitions,' Norbert said. 'They don't bite now. Promise.'

Hilton gave a huge sigh and held out his hands while the jumpy little individual was placed into his upturned palms. It squiggled and squirmed around, sniffing the air, its whiskers brushing Hilton's skin, producing the most miniscule electric shocks. Suddenly, its tiny wet nose touched him, and he flinched, afraid of the bite to follow. He started to giggle when a pink tongue, no longer than his little fingernail flicked out and started to lick his skin.

It felt divine. He was back in squirrel territory.

'I could say he was apologising for his grandad biting you,' Uncle Norbert laughed, 'but the truth is, he likes the salt in your sweaty palms.'

Hilton wiped his hand down the front of his trousers. 'Has Rodders ever won anything, Uncle? I mean...his eyes...does it matter? I thought the winners...well, ... they'd be the biggest or maybe the strongest ferrets, and that both eyes would have to be… you know…*the same colour?*'

'When I took my first look I knew he'd win nothing, son, but he's a big character. Wins the personality competition every time,' Uncle Norbert said. 'Let's crack onto Crocus Cottage, meet some more. Don't fret about being bitten though. That's one thing I *have* got right.'

INSIDE EACH SHED, THERE WERE oodles of ferrets, too many to count.

Some were brown and white, some totally white, the odd black one. Lots had light-coloured bodies and darker legs. Some were fully grown with the same number of little ones scampering around. There was movement all around as the creatures wriggled happily, dodging over, around, and under one another.

The thing Hilton noticed most in every shed was… *that smell.*

It wafted towards him. The cloud of odious odour formed itself invisibly into a big fat boxing glove which Hilton imagined would have a punch like a prize fighter. It drifted closer and landed a blow between Hilton's eyes. It made them water and he coughed to clear his throat.

His uncle didn't seem to notice.

As Hilton looked more closely at the creatures, he thought their fur a little mangey, and their eyes a little dull, even though they scuttled and cavorted around like furry ninjas.

'Uncle Norbert…' he said, being very polite in his wording, '…is there a bit of a ……'

'A pong, lad?' the old man said. 'We can do baths more often now there's two of us.'

'They get in the bath with you, Uncle?'

Norbert tutted. 'There's a couple of things you need to know. No matter how you try, you'll never stop them digging the food out of their bowls. Little blighters can't keep them tidy. I've tried everything but diving in to the bottom and throwing it all out onto the floor seems to be programmed into them. Bit like you, when you were in your high chair.'

The pair moved on, checking each of the animals. Every single one had a name and Norbert recognised them all. Gladys and Cassidy. Elton and Cilla.

Hilton would never learn all their names.

'Was there more I needed to know?' Hilton asked. 'You said, a couple of things.'

'Apparently, I'm told that they chatter and hiss when they're afraid. I've never heard it. But, remember Hilton, and this is *really* important, whenever you handle them, what you *must* do is keep the males and females apart.' He pointed to the fences constructed in each shed, creating a barrier down the middle. 'Hobs, that's the males, to the right side, jills to the left. And *don't* go mixing them up. We've enough mouths to feed.'

'How've you got so many, Uncle?'

'They're cunning little beggars,' Norbert said. 'They can chew their way through anything. The odd one will find a way under, over or through, and then, *you know...*' And he did his little whistley thing.

'Why don't you keep the hobs and jills in separate sheds?' Hilton checked.

'Where would be the fun in that, lad?' the old man asked, shrugging his shoulders.

'TIME FOR A BITE... *to eat*, I mean, Hilton,' his uncle joked. 'Then, ring your mum and dad. Tell them you're settled. We'll take Rodney and a couple of his mates out for a stroll along the lane before it gets dark. Maybe Winifred and Sigmund, they're his best pals.'

'Don't they run off, Uncle Norbert, when you take them from their sheds?'

'Don't be daft, lad. Not wearing their harnesses and leads.'

Chapter Five – A Ferreting Failure

'I've been meaning to ask,' Hilton said next morning, as they sat together for breakfast. Rodney was running playfully and hopping nimbly onto the workbench. The little animal pushed at a box of Snowy Flakes until it toppled over, the contents spilling like a crunchy waterfall across the table. Rodders sniffed pickily at the cereal, flicking the pieces from the bench with the tip of his nose.

'He likes Oaty Flakes for breakfast,' Uncle Norbert sighed. 'Keep him away from that telephone, lad. They're little devils if they get hold of a cable. *And, you know* how sharp their teeth are.'

Hilton could feel his colour drain.

'Go on lad, you were saying....'

'Your sign at the end of the lane, says 'Boarding and Welfare Society'. What does that mean, exactly?'

'When people go on holiday, I look after their ferrets. The boarding bit's in Apple Blossom Bungalow. And the Welfare part? Well, I was considered a bit of an expert back in the day. Used to sell them, give talks, help ferret folk with all sorts of things.'

'What do you mean, "used to"?' Hilton asked. 'You don't do it any longer?'

'Trouble is,' the old man continued, 'Horace Huxley up at Spine Acre Farm, he's the one they go to now. Wins all the competitions, you see. Best ferrets in the whole of Northumbria. The smartest, most handsome and the sweetest smelling, he says.'

Uncle Norbert went on to tell the boy about the ferret competitions he entered every so often. People built agility runs, he said, collecting tubes and ladders and see-saws to create circuits the ferrets could complete against the clock, a bit like the dog show Hilton had watched on TV. Ferrets could come when called, like dogs, his uncle explained, although he'd never managed to train his own to do that. And they could win awards for almost everything, like The Longest Body, The Reddest Eyes and The Best Working Pair.

Ferret competitions sounded about the best thing in the whole, wide world, Hilton thought. Games and ferrets. Games with ferrets. Games for ferrets. Prizes and money to be won.

The perfect combination.

'When's the next one, Uncle?' he asked.

'Don't go getting all excited, lad. No-one gets a look-in now Huxley scoops all the awards. The odd thing is, and keep this under your hat, he started his empire by stealing the original Rodney. *He* was my best ferret, ever.'

'Didn't you go to the police?'

The old man laughed. 'For a ferret? He was sneaky, you know. There was nothing I could prove.'

Uncle Norbert suspected Huxley had switched ferrets at the end of the competitions, taking Rodney, and leaving another hob the same colour and size but who wasn't Rodney at all. He only discovered this when his animals were returned to their cages at Bluebell Lodge.

'Nothing to be done about it now. First things first, let's pop to Bingley's, get enough ferret food 'til I can arrange my usual delivery of Merlin's Miracle. We're running very low.'

HILTON LOVED GOING TO BINGLEY'S superstore. They sold everything and he'd been lots of times, buying the wallpaper his mum loved

17

but dad hated, and then new cups and plates he chose for the kitchen. Nice ones, with animal pictures only he liked.

'We'll take Rodders along,' Uncle Norbert said. 'He likes a look out.'

'On his harness and lead?' Hilton checked.

'Don't be daft, lad. In his special carrier.'

Chapter Six – Bother at Bingley's

RODDERS' SPECIAL TRANSPORT RESEMBLED A cat carrier shrunk in the wash.

Made of moulded white plastic, everyone could see the ferret loved being inside. He poked his nose through the wire grid at the front, and his whiskers wiggled as he sniffed the air.

Once the uncle and nephew locked the car and headed towards Bingley's main entrance, Rodders' nose and whiskers resembled tiny aeroplane propellers, twisting and vibrating at speed. His pink tongue popped out of his mouth as if tasting the air, and his beady eyes were fixed on where Uncle Norbert was taking him.

'He's been before. They've got decent pet supplies here, and Rodders loves coming out in the sun.'

It was another glorious summer day, and Hilton was happy to escape the Fragrance of Ferret hanging heavily over the sheds.

A couple of people caught Hilton's eye, looked at him, then his uncle, then looked away. Hilton wasn't sure why.

Was it the way the old man dressed, his cordless cords and spaghetti wool jumper, or the caged ferret that caught their attention?

'DON'T THEY KNOW IT'S THE middle of August?' his uncle complained, as they walked down a long aisle, passing a huge display of things for Christmas. White, green and black tinsel trees on stands decorated the aisle, laden with baubles that glistened and twirled, strings of fairy lights shaped like butterflies, and pretty frosted lanterns. Rows of garlands and wreaths in greens and silvers, reds and golds filled the fixtures.

Everything seemed to sparkle.

Hilton looked down at his feet where a thin layer of glittery particles had fallen. The aisle was illuminated by a shaft of sunlight, and twinkly flecks stuck to the soles of their shoes as they walked, leaving imprints where they'd been.

'You'd not see *his* prints down there, they're so tiny,' Hilton said, pointing to Rodders.

'Bad combination, ferrets and glitter,' Uncle Norbert grumbled. 'It'll get into their fur. Where is the Blaze's Best?'

In the pet food aisle, Hilton and his uncle scanned the shelves until they found the large green sacks, each with a picture of the cutest, whitest ferret printed on the side.

BLAZE'S BEST.

BEST FOR YOUR FERRET, BEST FOR YOU.

'You take Rodders, son. I'll bring the sacks,' Norbert said, putting down the carrier onto the ground.

The tills were busy. While they waited, Hilton could feel Rodders scampering around inside his transport, darting to one side then the other, the weight shifting front to back, this side then that, as he flitted around to see what was happening.

In the queue, the lady before them had a trolley full of Christmas things. It was overloaded and a box slid from the pile, landing with a clatter on the floor.

Being short, she struggled to reach down and control the trolley at the same time. She puffed as her fringe of short brown hair flapped in the way, ending beyond her eyebrows, merging with her tiny dark eyes. She raised her pointed nose aloft as she turned to the pair and picked up the box.

'My goodness!' she said in mousy exasperation. *Common shrew, Sorex araneus, page 15. Active by day* (definitely) *and night* (possibly*), they are very territorial and aggressive for their size* (let's hope not to find out) *and can sometimes be heard fighting, their high-pitched squeaks particularly noticeable during the summer.*

'I do apologise- this might take a while,' she said, nodding at the brimming trolley. She explained she would have to take Christmas things with her when she moved abroad next month. You couldn't buy decorations out there, she said.

The till beeped loudly as she continued to lift each item from the trolley and place them carefully on the counter, ready to be scanned. One by one, they were processed.

Six-foot white tinsel tree. BEEP.

Fairy lights, white. BEEP.

Baubles, assorted, 100. BEEP.

The flashing red light of the scanner continued as the woman organised one purchase after another onto the counter for the assistant to swipe. Rodders stared intently.

Treetop star, silver. BEEP.

Wreath, cones and acorns. BEEP.

And finally, she pulled from the bottom of the trolley a long garland, covered in icy-looking glitter. It shed a snowfall of sparkles as she pulled it free from the wire bars.

Mistletoe garland. BEEP.

'Who'd want that, with all the kissing malarkey?' Uncle Norbert sneered.

The lady blushed and quickly packed it back into her trolley which was now overflowing with glitzy goods.

Hilton elbowed his uncle and looked at the counter. 'Look at all the glitter,' he said. The lady paid and pushed the heavy trolley towards the exit, walking on her tiptoes, and leaning over it with her arms outstretched to keep her Christmas decorations under control.

It was their turn, at last. The till assistant held up her hand.

'One moment sir, I've been told to clean down the counter when it gets messy, you know, with glitter or soil and the like.'

In the heat, she pushed back her long grey hair, tied flat to her head in a ponytail, beads of perspiration rolling down her brow towards her big brown eyes. *Grey seal* (perhaps?). *Halichoerus grypus, page 39. Grey seals' hands and feet are formed into webbed flippers* (not this one) *and they have no visible ears* (true). *Their scientific name derives from the Greek for 'hook-nosed sea pig'.*

As he studied her face carefully for any evidence of a hooknose, she removed from beneath the counter a large wide paintbrush and used it, rather like a flipper he thought, to sweep glitter from the surface, flick, flick, flicking it away. But, oddly, Hilton realised as he watched, she was doing it in the wrong direction, cleaning it outward, towards him and his uncle, not down the counter and away from the shoppers. Hilton was fascinated, and his eyes stuck firmly to the bristles of the paintbrush as the worker swept.

The sun was streaming through Bingley's large windows. It lit up every individual sparkly particle, creating an airborne stream of glitter suspended in front of them, headed slowly in their direction.

At that very moment, an odd thing happened. Everything went quiet.

As the glitter twinkled and fluttered around them, the man standing behind, who had been laughing out loud, stopped suddenly. His face was stuck in a forced laughing expression that looked quite scary as there was no noise coming from his mouth. His bulbous tongue was bigger than the size of Rodders' head, and a sprinkling of toast crumbs, possibly today's, or worse, yesterday's, decorated his moustache.

Everything was still. The music that had been playing in the background stopped. The till assistant had come to a halt, paintbrush poised on the counter. Hilton looked up at Uncle Norbert.

The same had happened to him. He was frozen.

His expression, and the way he stood with his hand in his pocket waiting to pay for the Blaze's Best, totally stalled. Hilton cast his eyes along the row of tills. The same thing was happening everywhere.

It was most strange.

Everything was at a complete standstill, except for him and the cascade of silver glinting strands. He looked into Rodney's carrier. The little creature was locked in position at the mesh door, looking out, eyes and whiskers unmoving.

Around the boy, his uncle, and the ferret, the flakes of glitter twirled and travelled in the rays of sunshine that illuminated the whole scene.

Chapter Seven – A Sprinkling of Glitter

'THAT'S QUITE SOME SPRINKLING OF pixie dust, mate!' the man behind said, smiling at the sparkles now decorating Norbert's head and shoulders.

The music restarted. Everything clicked back into life as quickly as it had stopped.

'Ooh, sorry!' the till lady said, getting a bit flustered. 'I just wasn't thinking….' She started to flap her hands around Uncle Norbert, trying to remove some of the glints shining in his hair and on his face.

'Pfffff,' he said, wafting away the assistant's help in a cross sort of way.

Hilton scratched his head. He couldn't understand. Why had everything paused at that very twinkly moment?

As Uncle Norbert spat out little flakes of glitter that had landed on his lips and flicked pieces out from his eyebrows, he scratched around in his pockets to find enough to pay for the sacks of ferret food now on the counter. 'Bloomin' stuff!' he grumbled. 'Wipe it off, before we get outside, lad. Don't want people to be staring at us.'

Hilton collected the till receipt and looked down at Rodney, happily scampering to and fro inside the carrier again. The boy ran his hand through his hair to make sure it was glitter-free as they set off towards the car park.

Uncle Norbert balanced the sacks on his left shoulder and jangled the car keys in his hand. Rodney's carrier swung gently in the warm breeze as they got in, ready for the journey home.

Hilton listened as the bigger bushes scraped the outside of the car as it squeezed up the narrow lane. He winced, knowing the scuffing noises would turn into scratches. My dad would go mad if this were *his* car, he thought.

But the only thing Uncle Norbert seemed to worry about, ever, was his ferrets. Not the house. Not himself.

And certainly not his car.

'Blaze's Best is pretty good,' the old man said, pulling the sacks up to stand in the corner of his bedroom when they were home. 'But Merlin's Miracle is definitely best. It's the one I've used for years.'

Hilton cast his eyes around the room.

A thick layer of dust had gathered over many years, encrusting the surface of a chest of drawers. The bed had woollen blankets with a selection of coffee-coloured stains, resembling a map of the world, and a sharp metal spring was escaping from the bare mattress. It looked like a steel snake. Possibly an adder, *Vipera berus, page 44.*

'Doesn't that stick in you, Uncle?' he asked, pointing to the silvery coil poking angrily through the fabric.

The old man looked at Hilton, and then at the bed. 'Doesn't bother me since, you know…. your Aunt Izolda….' His voice trailed off.

Hilton knew it was best to leave the spring-thing alone. He changed the subject, like he'd watched his dad do when his mum rolled her eyes or tutted. 'Maybe it's time to switch their food. Might bring you fresh luck. My dad's always saying that.'

'Aye lad, perhaps you're right. Something's got to change, that's for sure. There's not enough coming in from the boarding to keep these animals in the best way. Let's get Rodders back. Then we can have a cuppa.'

As the pair made their way through the ramshackle sheds, each one with its own bit of roof or wall dangling in the breeze, Hilton held his nose. The ferret smell was really strong today and it stung like someone had set fire to the hairs inside his nostrils.

'I'll show you the bathing tomorrow,' Uncle Norbert said. 'I've a special shed with everything we need. You'll love to watch them swim in the tin tub. Here Rodders, you're home.'

Bluebell Lodge had a smell that made Hilton's eyes burn.

'You do the handling, son,' Norbert said. 'Open the carrier… a calming stroke… that's right… then, when you're ready, pop him in his enclosure.'

Hilton was relieved when Rodders behaved. The boy stood next to the wire barrier that ran down the middle of the hut.

'Ah, he's got glitter all over him,' Hilton said, stroking the creature's fur and trying to flick off the shiny particles determined to stay exactly where they were. He puffed and blew at Rodders, ruffling his fur, seeing down to the dainty pink skin below, and secretly hoping he wouldn't frighten him.

'He's first for the tub tomorrow. Just pop him back. What's the time now?' the old man asked. Hilton leaned forward, Rodders perched in his cupped hands. He let go gently, and the little animal scurried off.

'Ah Hilton, what did I say? You've put him in the *female* side with the jills. Get him out. QUICK!'

But Rodders, the only sparkly ferret in the whole of the East Northumbria Ferret Boarding and Welfare Society, was not about to be removed. He cavorted through the girls' pen, giving Hilton and Norbert the slip at every twist and turn, flashing and glistening as he scuttled around.

The old man called out. 'Glynis, Mabel, Elsa! Out of his way if you know what's good for you!'

'The glitter's gone to his head,' Norbert said, as they eventually retrieved Rodney from the jills' pen, happy that all he had done was run around and frighten the girls a little.

'That's where you belong, lad,' Norbert tutted, setting the ferret down into the right side of the shed. The old man and boy patted one another on the back, happy to get Rodders back to the hobs as soon as they could. 'Trying to impress the lasses with his sparkles,' Norbert laughed. 'Something to tell your mum and dad tonight. It's time you called home.'

ON THE FRONT DOORMAT LAY two letters addressed to Mr Norbert Norris, one in a beige envelope stamped Northumbria and North East Ferret Society and the other in a white envelope from Heslop's Bank.

'Not much point in opening either,' Norbert sighed, hanging his cap on a large black nail sticking out of the cracked wall.

Over tea, he read out the letter from the ferret society. Bagley Festival of Ferrets was taking place soon, it said, and invited him to register animals into a wide range of competitions, and to please send the entry fees.

'Sounds really cool,' Hilton said, already planning which event the Bluebell Lodge ferrets might do well at.

'Trouble is,' his uncle said, 'it's a waste of fees when Horace Huxley wins everything. No wonder he's making money hand over fist. Everyone wants to buy his winners.'

It had been a busy and a very strange day, one way and another. The uncle and nephew decided to sleep on it, and the next morning agreed on a small number of ferrets to enter into the festival, just to give the horrible Huxley some competition, and Rodders another day out.

Chapter Eight – All That Glitters

NEXT DAY, AT THE DOOR of Bluebell Lodge, Hilton started to sniff. He expected *that* smell.

He took in several slow nostrils full. Something had changed. He squinted as the door swung open. Yes, all the creatures were there.

'Uncle Norbert! Can you smell that?' he shouted, tugging at his uncle's raggy cardigan.

'Can't smell a thing,' he replied.

'That's it!' Hilton said. 'There *is* no smell!'

Together, they looked around, shaking their heads. The bedding was fresh, the water was clean, and their food was in the bowl, not on the floor. The ferrets were playing happily and came to the wire mesh to sniff Hilton's hands. Their eyes were bright and beady, and their coats gleamed in the shaft of light through the open door. Their happy squeaks created ferrety tunes which made Uncle Norbert laugh and clap his hands together.

'It's a long time since they've looked on such good form,' he nodded. 'I've given them Blaze's Best in the past, but it didn't have quite *this* effect.'

They stood together a watched for a while as the creatures played, rolling and toying with one another. Then, something caught Hilton's eye.

Mixed in the bedding on the shed floor were lots of bright strands, fragments of the sparkling glitter swept over the three of them at Bingley's yesterday. Odd flecks lay mixed in with the wood chippings and shone brilliantly, caught in the sunshine.

The ferrets had been at their busy best during the night, squiggling and squirming through the sparkly, woody mixture. The harder he concentrated, the clearer he could see. Every one of them had been in contact with it, each sporting the weeniest sparkle of glitter dust in their fur somewhere.

It made Hilton wonder. He pondered the odd happening at Bingley's yesterday, and whether the glitter might be connected. It was worth a try, he thought.

While Uncle Norbert was changing the water bottle, Hilton filled his hands with the floor sweepings and stuffed the glittery shavings into both trouser pockets. He dusted off the excess so his uncle wouldn't see.

The old man pulled open the shed door, ready to check the rest of the ferret houses. 'Either my nose has gone on strike or the air's fresher today, lad.'

Hilton had to agree. For the first time, there was no foul ferret smell in Bluebell Lodge and the creatures were on good form.

Was this the effect of the Blaze's Best?

Chapter Nine – Spreading the Love

AS THEY OPENED THE DOORS to the rest of the sheds Uncle Norbert secured so very carefully each night, the familiar smell reached out. It was strong and felt like a slap across Hilton's face. It stuck in the back of his throat.

'Gruuuuuuwww, Uncle,' Hilton said. 'I bet your nose is working now.'

'Just a ...just a minute, lad. Hear that?' Norbert said, holding up his hand to cup his ear.

Back at the house, Uncle Norbert's phone wasn't mobile at all. It was big and cream and very loud. It had one of those extra noisy bells put up outside in a big white plastic box on the wall so it echoed, and he could hear it ring whether he was in Bluebell Lodge or Apple Blossom Bungalow. It rang and rang and rang until Norbert lumbered off past the sheds and burst through the front door to silence it, muttering about how the boarding ferrets should've been collected earlier, and leaving Hilton straggling behind.

For a few moments, the boy was alone amidst the ferret housing. What if his theory about the special shiny flakes *was* correct?

He backtracked quickly into the rest of the sheds, sprinkling a little of the dusty glitter from his pockets, just a pinch here, a flake there, pretty much everywhere on the way back to the house.

ONCE THE CHORES WERE DONE, the dirty bedding raked out and replaced, the water bottles cleaned and refilled and the dishes topped up with Blaze's Best, the two could stroke and play with their furry family. Every single ferret, young or old, big or small, nosey or shy had a name, and Uncle Norbert knew them all. He cast his eye around the enclosures and pondered who should be bathed first.

'We'll do Neville, Ogden, Jagger and Wilbur, then come back for the jills,' he decided.

'Bagley Ferret Festival is next week, Uncle,' Hilton began. 'Shall we, err….I mean……Should we, err… send in our entries?'

Chapter Ten – The Morrisons Visit

MR AND MRS MORRISON TOOK an extraordinary length of time to collect their ferrets when they called for Jasper and Jonty later that afternoon.

The six of them, the two ferrets in their luxurious carrier complete with purple velvet cushion, the Morrisons, Uncle Norbert, and Hilton sat around the kitchen table for a long while, drinking tea and talking about the ferret festival happening soon.

Both Morrisons wore beige. He had a raincoat with brown edging while Mrs Morrison wore a quilted jacket with brown patch pockets. Scanning down, Hilton could see their large feet beneath the table, wearing matching brown brogues, highly polished with laces neatly tied. They looked at one another tenderly with big, brown eyes, chatting about events at Bingley's and laughing at the idea of Norbert covered in glitter.

As if, they said.

Hilton enjoyed studying the wildlife at close quarters.

Very social animals, fallow deer, Dama dama, page 21. With a keen sense of smell (too polite to mention it) *and large cupped ears able to rotate* (must watch for that), *they have a keen ability to recognise danger* (not needed in East Northumbria). *An identifying feature is their prominent Adam's apple* (not the female, in this instance) *and the buck's coat turns grey in winter* (very probably). *They leave large prints, making them easy to track* (confirmed).

Horace Huxley and his animals would win the competitions. Everyone knew that, they agreed.

The Morrisons had kept ferrets for a very long time, they told Hilton, and had bought theirs from Uncle Norbert when he was at the top of his game. Every one of his creatures won prizes at festivals across the north east.

'Those were the days,' his uncle said wistfully lifting up his spectacles and wiping his eyes, 'until it all went wrong. It was around the time your aunt....' The old man stared through a little cloud of sad moisture.

Mrs Morrison came to his rescue. 'Here's your chance to show Huxley you're still in the ferret game,' she said. 'We've entered Jasper into The Longest Whiskers and Jonty into the Agility Section. He likes a good run around Bagley Arena, does Jonty. Remember when he got out the last time?' She raised her eyebrows.

'Was that when he ran up the judge's skirt?' Norbert winked.

Hilton possibly had a great idea to try at school when he returned next month.

Or maybe not.

As the Morrison's car eventually pulled out of the lane, Uncle Norbert took the envelope marked Northumbria and North East Ferret Society from the kitchen drawer.

'This is who we should enter, lad,' he said. 'Tell me if you agree.'

Chapter Eleven – The Benefits of Blaze's Best

'BATH DAY TODAY AND NO excuses,' Uncle Norbert said, as he washed the breakfast dishes, leaving darker patches on his brown cord trousers where he wiped his wet hands. A little fluff of washing up bubbles stuck to the material. It resembled a cluster of frogspawn to Hilton, and he started to count in his head, checking how many 'eggs' were within. Seven, eight, nine.

'Happy with the festival entries, then?' the old man asked.

The frogspawn bubbles were still there, hanging on. So cool, frogs.

Rana temporia, the common frog, page 2. Frogs have an odd way of swallowing food; they actually use their eyes as part of the process. When they blink, it pushes their eyeballs down to create a bulge in the roof of their mouth. This pressure helps squeeze food down through the back of their throat.

'Seventeen…eighteen…' Hilton continued, only just catching what his uncle had said.

'Eighteen? I can't afford to enter eighteen, Hilton!'

'Sorry, Uncle, I was erm… working out… how many days 'til school restarts,' he lied. 'Your ferrets all have a good chance the way things are going.' He glanced at the completed form heading soon to the ferret society, giving details of Norbert's selection into the event next week.

'Ogden in the Agility....yep, he's very ...erm....bendy, and Neville in The Longest Whiskers, I agree. Mabel in The Maze? She's clever, that girl, and Rubina in the ferret Grand National race. She's superfast. Perfect!' he said, glancing sideways at his uncle's trousers.

Most of the bubbles had gone.

'Let's hope everything smells like Bluebell Lodge did yesterday,' the boy said, as they collected the feed and headed to the back door. 'You first, Uncle,' Hilton gestured, picking up a bucket brimming with the beige pellets of Blaze's Best.

'School will like the new-improved manners when you go back, son,' the old man said, unaware Hilton was still counting under his breath, watching the clinging frogspawn.

BLUEBELL LODGE SMELLED GOOD, AND Hilton watched the beautiful little bendy buses at play. Their dark eyes shone like black diamonds. Today, their glossy coats lay flat and smooth against their firm bodies highlighting the colours; the pure white, the sandy, the copper shades. The prize-*worthy* ferrets *were* looking even better than yesterday, Hilton thought, and he returned to his glitter-spreading theory.

What else could explain the changes?

He imagined himself with a pink wet nose and wiggly whiskers, magnifying glass in paw, becoming a Great Ferret Detective. More evidence would be needed before sharing his thoughts with Uncle Norbert.

Crocus Cottage was next, and they threw open the rickety door. As it flapped in the breeze, squeaking on rusty hinges, the pair took a deep breath, expecting to have the insides of their nostrils peeled by the smell.

Cautiously, they took one step inside. Then another. And one more.

They looked at each other. 'Uncle?'

'I know what you're about to say, lad.'

'Not there, is it? The smell, I mean,' Hilton said, scratching his head.

'No, but *you've still* got glitter in your hair,' the old man said distractedly, puffing at a gleam of silver on Hilton's head. He tried to flick out the shiny sparkle with his fingers. 'Need to have a bath of your own, son.'

'I'm getting to like pixie dust, Uncle,' he said. 'Maybe it'll bring us luck.'

'It'll bring *you* a phone call from your dad when I tell him you're not getting washed properly,' Norbert said.

Hilton ran his eyes slowly over his untidy and definitely whiffy ferret-partner-of-an-uncle, the grey messy hair and bristly unshaven face, the jumper splodged with milk stains from this morning's breakfast and his boots covered in ferret unmentionables.

'I can't imagine where you get your fear of water,' the old man smirked as he reached into a pen full of jills and picked up the first animal that sniffed at him. 'Look how beautiful *she* is!' he said. 'There's no smell in here either. Maybe I'll change to Blaze's Best permanently. Seems to agree with them.'

Chapter Twelve – Getting Ready for Bagley Ferret Festival

THE TIN BATH WAS FULL of warm, soapy water. Hilton watched his uncle swish the bubbles around evenly with his big badger hands covered in coarse grey hairs. His nails were filthy, and really rather like claws, but their daily jobs did include scratching out all the dirty ferret bedding and digging to the very bottom of each feed sack to make sure nothing was wasted.

Norbert reached for an apron hanging on the back of the shed door. It was blue and frilly and secured with long strings of navy twisted cord, but there was something about the way the old man lifted it tenderly from its hook, smoothed away its creases one by one and patted it over his own body that showed Hilton it was special.

He nodded respectfully at his uncle. 'Cool,' he said. 'What happens next?'

'We'll put Ogden and Neville in together. The girls can stay in the pen 'til they're ready. Got their favourite things to play with.'

'Balls?' Hilton asked.

'Hammocks.'

'….Pardon, Uncle?'

Norbert pointed to the cage on the floor where a ferret-sized yellow hammock was slung like a fabric banana between its wire bars, secured with thin, black ties. 'They love it. Just watch.'

Hilton's eyes were glued on the furry cat-snakes.

Mabel and Rubina appeared to be having a ferret conversation about who should have the hammock first. Mabel wound her way beneath the yellow sling, and placed her front paws on its side, tipping it towards her body. As it rolled slightly, she hopped in and turned around quick as a flash, ending up on her back like a hairy sun worshipper on a deck chair. She knew exactly how to twist her long body to make the hammock swing, but as she lay, Rubina was becoming impatient and pawed at the hammock edge to tilt it again, rolling Mabel clean out onto the floor. With a swift hop, she took up the same position Mabel had left, and lay triumphantly on her coppery back.

All that was needed to complete the scene, Hilton thought, was a pair of ferret sunglasses. Watching their pretty panda faces swinging happily was better than any summer holiday he could ever imagine.

After a few swings, Mabel was back, claiming her place on the yellow hammock, and so the jills went on. There was no squawking or nipping, just good tempered, ferrety fun. Hilton found it hard to concentrate on anything else.

Using his bar of fur-friendly soap, and a little jug of clean water to rinse when they were done, Uncle Norbert gave Hilton a step-by-step guide to the art of ferret-bathing. Ogden demonstrated his powers as a super-swimmer as he happily doggy-paddled, or more accurately, ferret-paddled around the edge of the tin bath.

Norbert carefully soaped up Neville, then rinsed him clean, eventually putting him into the blue frilly apron which acted as a wet ferret hammock between his knees. He dried off the skinny, drenched body and passed him to Hilton who was armed with an old and slightly threadbare blue towel.

'She liked blue, your Aunt Izolda,' Norbert said, thoughtfully.

If I did this with Mum's towels, she'd go spare, Hilton thought, knowing that Uncle Norbert didn't care about towels; blue, threadbare, or otherwise.

Just ferrets.

'When he's dry enough, you can deliver him straight back to Bluebell Lodge,' Norbert said. 'He's got a big day tomorrow. But don't forget, put him in…'

'…with the hobs, not the jills. Yes, *I know.*'

Hilton used his gentlest touch to pat the water from Neville who was nestled inside the towel making happy squeaks while the boy whispered to him. 'You *have* got the longest whiskers Neville, and if I didn't know better, I'd say they're even longer today!'

WITH THE FERRET FIVE CLEAN and returned to Bluebell Lodge, Uncle Norbert tipped away the dirty ferret-water outside the shed door.

'The entry fees have been received, and the festival starts at one o'clock tomorrow,' he said. 'Let's have an early night, son.' He ruffled Hilton's hair. 'Maybe *you'll* be my lucky mascot.'

Chapter Thirteen – The Lucky Charm

As they pulled into Bagley Arena car park next day, Hilton felt nervous.

Uncle Norbert marched ahead with Ogden, Neville and Rodders together in the one travel cage, looking slightly squashed. 'I've a good feeling about today, lad,' he kept saying.

Hilton scurried behind with the carton holding Mabel and Rubina. It was a large cardboard box previously containing Ferra-Vite vitamins but was now full of air holes punctured by Norbert's screwdriver. A bungee held the lid in place. Balancing the box to keep the jills calm, he hurried to match his uncle's lumbering strides, but in the queue at the entrance, they bumped into the Morrisons, with their posh carrier and Jonty and Jasper curled up together inside.

Mrs Morrison looked at Norbert's neatly packed hobs and the big box Hilton was carrying. She pulled a quizzical sort of face.

'Mabel and Rubina,' Hilton explained, holding up the package and displaying the air holes.

A strangled tune escaped from a piper who appeared from nowhere, squeezing at bellows tucked under his arm. He walked proudly across the arena playing his Northumbrian pipes as the contestants followed behind with their animal carriers.

'Best of luck,' Mr Morrison said. 'Remember, you've as good a chance as anyone. Let's show Huxley who's boss in the ferret world!' He slapped Hilton's uncle on the back and the ferret cage swung a little out of control.

'Watch out Morris! I need everything going for me, today. But I've my lucky charm here,' Norbert said, nodding his head towards Hilton, 'and he's *even* had a bath, especially.'

Hilton blushed. Because that was true. Or maybe because his theory about their 'luck' was about to be tested.

Mrs Morrison peered inside Rodders' carrier. 'What are you doing different, Norbert?' she asked, squinting at the three males. 'They're looking top notch today, and they smell …. beautiful.'

'Don't encourage him too much, Doris,' her husband said. 'We're in competition with him, remember.'

At a table just inside the door, Hilton and his uncle rested their loads.

'We'll have to split up, lad. Too many events at the same time.' He pointed to the far side of the hall.

'You take the girls. I'll have the boys. Just do what I showed you. You'll be fine. There's an award for Best Junior Handler. If we get nothing else, *you* might be lucky.'

The old man patted the top of Hilton's head, messing up his neat blond hair. 'Aw lad, you might have had a bath, but there's still flakes of that bloomin' stuff in your mop.'

Hilton knew. He felt very happy.

Chapter Fourteen – Fighting Talk at the Ferret Festival

At the Maze event, the judge towered over a large wooden maze placed on the table top. It was full of narrow little alleyways which seemed to go nowhere. He held up a large, black stopwatch for everyone to see.

Hilton held Mabel under her front legs, her bottom half resting in his upturned palm like a big furry paintbrush, as his uncle had taught him. He could feel her quick heartbeat banging away like the engine in Uncle Norbert's car, but his heart was working harder. He breathed in deeply, listening carefully as the judge explained the rules.

'You're last to go, son. When I give the signal, put the jill in where it says 'Start'. I'll count you down. We've had some quick rounds already. Three, two, one. *Go!*'

Mabel hadn't seen a maze before, but Hilton watched the little girl sniff the air and flick her tongue as she got on with her important work. Her head weaved side to side as she scuttled and ran, reversed and turned.

Hilton's heart clanged in his chest as the furry little creature scampered its way up this alley inside the maze, to the left, then the right, and stopped for a moment.

Come on Mabel! Hilton thought. Use your nose. *Hurry!*

Picking up the scent, she scurried through the narrow lanes of the maze, the speedy movement of her short legs hypnotising Hilton until the judge's whistle blew in his ear. It made him jump.

'Well, son, first time for you and the jill, you say? Ladies and gents, Mabel here, scored 19.5 seconds, putting her in *second* place!'

Everyone standing around the table clapped. Hilton felt about to burst.

He planted a kiss on Mabel's head and popped her back inside the box, looking next for the Ferret Grand National. As he searched, a man approached. He'd been standing at the Maze too, Hilton remembered.

But the stranger, tall and thin with jet black hair and dark hooded eyes, glowered at the boy, his face unmoving. His long body bent down and picked up a large carrier from the floor. It was covered in big yellow labels. *Huxley's- Northumbria's Number One for Ferrets*, they read.

As he moved closer, Hilton watched his expression become as stiff as stone. His look became more hateful, frightening the boy and making his chest feel tight as he took in every detail. Dressed in a grey jacket and black coat, he sported a white shirt and yellow tie and had one foot propped on the wall behind, creating an equilateral triangle of leg and wall. His overlong black hair was slicked back and his nose long and crooked.

That is one big-billed bird, Hilton thought. *Stork, Ciconia ciconiidae, page 44?* Too slim. *Egret, Egretta garzetta, page 41?* Or... Hilton's mind raced over the well-thumbed pages of the book burned deep into his memory.

'You the kid helping Norbert?' the man checked. He looked around to make sure no-one was listening. 'Be happy with second place 'cos *my* ferrets are Number One around here.'

Hilton's tummy hit the ground. He couldn't speak. Or control his jelly-legs.

Ardea cinereal, grey heron, page 37. Stands stock still, often on one leg (he did), *waiting patiently for its catch* (not today, thank you), *the grey heron has a strong build and dagger-like beak. This solitary predator feasts on rodents, fish and has even been known to consume the occasional duckling* (what sort of creature steals an innocent baby duckling?).

SOMEHOW, HILTON'S LEGS WOBBLED HIM across to the Grand National course. Like the horse races his dad watched, this had long lanes, one for each ferret, with little fences for the animals to jump as they ran along the floor.

Standing at the winning post, looking down the length of the racetrack, was Huxley. He smiled at everyone who passed, but when no-one was near, he'd look up and snarl at Hilton, pulling sharp faces at the box containing Mabel and Rubina.

Mr Morrison sidled up to Hilton. 'He's a nasty sly piece of work,' he said. 'Wants everyone to think he's nice as pie, but if you've good ferrets, he's out for blood.'

Hilton swallowed. Mr Morrison watched the boy's colour drain from his face. He patted Hilton's arm. 'Not real blood, son. But, he *is* desperate to win. There's a lot at stake, being at the top of the ferret world.'

Suddenly, a loud whistle was blown, and the judge shouted. 'Competitors to the start. We are ready.'

Mr Morrison sandwiched himself between the little blond Hilton and the tall, dark spiky figure of Huxley. 'You'll be okay now,' he whispered.

'Competitors! Put down your ferrets….and, on my signal, three, two, one. *Go!*'

Inside the hall, there was an explosion of noise, encouragement from the excited owners as the flexible tubes of fur raced their way along the course, jumping over hurdles and boxes.

Hilton was tracking every ferret across the lanes and quickly lost sight of Rubina. 'I ....I ...can't....can't see...her,' he said to Mr Morrison.

'There she is now, coming over the green hedge!'

The judge's whistle sounded, and his voice boomed across the hall. 'And the winner is lane number six, Rubina. Owner, Norbert Norris.' A huge cheer rang around the hall.

'It's time someone other than Huxley won,' someone said to Hilton, patting him on the back as he picked up Rubina from the end of the course.

The judge held up his hand. 'Back to the main arena please. All events are completed now.'

Among the huddle of competitors, Hilton eventually found his uncle.

'You'll *never* guess, Uncle Norbert....' he breathed, desperate to share the good news, but was quickly hushed by the old man.

'No son, *you'll* never guess...'he said, putting his finger on Hilton's lips.

Chapter Fifteen – A Really Nice Man

THE PANEL OF JUDGES WAS gathered at the prize table. It groaned under the weight of trophies and medals to be presented. Around the hall, the owners sat with carriers by their sides, all types, but Hilton was the only person with a box full of holes. Sitting in front of Uncle Norbert was Huxley with his carrier, much bigger than anyone else's, two separate levels, a ferret upstairs and downstairs, and lined with fur. A water bottle was suspended on the door with another of Huxley's stickers, claiming he was Northumbria's Number One for ferrets. He sat absolutely still, his neck outstretched, listening for the results.

Hilton nudged his uncle, pointing at the super-sized carrier. 'He might not be number one today,' the boy whispered. The Morrisons, sitting next to them agreed, nodding their heads, and shushing the boy to keep his voice down.

'Another brilliant turn-out,' the head judge said, rising to his feet. 'So, let's get started with the prize-winners.'

Hilton listened carefully and squinted in concentration as the result for each event was read out. 'My hands are stinging,' Hilton said, 'clapping for all these people.'

'They'll do the same when it's our turn, son,' his uncle said, tapping the boy's knee. 'Any time now, I reckon.' The Morrisons shot a glance across to his uncle and Hilton realised something was about to happen.

'And in the Hobs' Agility class, the winner is….Ogden, owned by Norbert Norris. Second is Jonty, owned by his best pal and rival, Morris Morrison.'

His uncle beamed as he shot from his chair and rushed forward to collect the gleaming cup from the judge. He slapped Morris on the back as they walked together. The clapping and cheering got louder, and Hilton was beginning to realise how many people in this furry, pear-shaped ferrety world liked his uncle. He cheered with them.

Huxley turned around. He scowled at the boy. 'Not so fast, blondie,' he snapped. 'There's more results to come.' He tapped the top of his carrier, keeping his cold dark eyes fixed on Hilton.

Hilton looked away from the fearful face. His gaze stopped on Huxley's reddened hands, his fingers covered in tiny, white raised scars. Ferret bites. Hilton could understand why his creatures would be afraid.

'Don't take any notice, Hilton,' Mrs Morrison said. 'He's got to win, at any cost.'

Today, Neville had been the ferret with The Longest Whiskers his uncle explained, as he pinned a winning green rosette onto his nephew's jumper. 'But, *you've* done all the hard work really, Uncle.'

'You and your glittery hair. You're my lucky mascot!' the old man smiled.

Maybe, Hilton thought.

'Second place in The Maze Competition, is Mabel…again, owned by Norbert Norris. And we're coming into the final couple of prizes, ladies and gentlemen. Next up, is winner of the Ferret Grand National.'

There was silence in the hall.

Hilton started to shuffle in his seat. He'd not had the chance to share the brilliant news about Rubina's nifty racing. But, before the judge could announce third, second and then Rubina as the winner, Huxley's cap of black hair rotated towards them again.

'Bit of a winning streak, eh?' he said, in a low, quiet voice meant for only Norbert and his nephew, but the Morrisons heard too.

Mrs Morrison leaned over. 'He's vicious that one, Norbert. Better watch out.'

'First place in the Grand National goes to... Rubina... Owner...' the judge started.

'*Norbert Norris! Hooray!*' the crowd shouted, clapping their hands and whooping. The uncle stepped forward to collect his trophy. This would be engraved with Rubina's name, the judge said, also handing him an envelope.

'Don't forget your prize money, Norbert,' he said. 'It's a long time since your animals did so well here.'

The two men shook hands for a very long while, and the Morrisons did the same to Hilton. His mouth was dry, and his head starting to buzz, in a good way.

'And the last prize, Best Junior Handler.' Everyone's eyes were on Hilton. 'A total newcomer but a natural with our furry friends. It's Hilton Hughes!'

Hilton felt himself grow by several metres or possibly just some millimetres. He was feeling on top of the world. He couldn't wait to get back and ring his mum and dad.

IT TOOK A LITTLE WHILE to get away from the ferret festival. People wanted to congratulate them, tell them it was great to see Norbert's ferrets back on form, and what a good help Hilton must be. A spreader of lucky glitter, he thought.

Almost everyone had drifted off. The pair were giving the Ferret Five treats of bananas and grapes, and packing away the trophies and rosettes in Hilton's rucksack, when Huxley stalked across the hall. He was smiling at everyone else, but the closer he got to the successful pair, the darker and more grim his face became.

Standing with his back to the few stragglers left, he spoke through gritted teeth. 'Not sure what's changed, *mate*,' he said, offering his hand for Norbert to shake, 'but, we could work together, me and you. A partnership of the best.'

Uncle Norbert ignored the outstretched hand and looked Huxley straight in the eye. 'No thanks, *mate*,' he said politely. 'You have your methods, I have mine. Let's leave it like that.'

'You'll regret that offer, you old fool,' Huxley muttered, turning to leave the hall, his face all smiles once more and his kneecaps clacking together.

Hilton's leg bones had jellified again. He held onto a chair to steady himself. 'Blimey, Uncle. He's a bit…'

'Two-faced, Hilton. That's what he is. I'd not trust him as far as I could throw a sack of Blaze's Best.'

Chapter Sixteen – A Visitor at Night

IT WAS QUITE A CELEBRATION back at the East Northumbria Ferret Boarding and Welfare Society.

Uncle Norbert stopped off at Rav's Chippy, and for the first time in weeks, Hilton enjoyed his tea. They chatted at the table devouring fat salty chips and fresh white cod, picking off flakes of the delicious brown batter. His uncle might be a great ferret-man, he thought, but he cooked like he cared for himself: not very well.

The ferrets were back in their sheds. The left-over banana and grape mixture was all gone, and Hilton had found a browning lettuce loitering in the fridge, which, once the outside leaves were peeled, was perfect for the hobs and the jills to share, celebrating the day's fantastic results.

HILTON WAS IN HIS PYJAMAS, ready for bed, when there was a rap at the door. 'Oh, it's you,' he heard his uncle say, in a strange tone Hilton didn't recognise. The old man shuffled back, opening the door a little wider but keeping the visitor outside.

Hilton couldn't see who it was or clearly hear what the man's voice was saying. 'Out of order….'he heard. 'Come to say sorry…'

The front door was opened fully and the man on the doorstep walked his knobbly knees in. It was Huxley.

Hilton drew in a large breath, remembering the last vicious words exchanged at the festival. 'Huxley realises he went a bit too far earlier,' Norbert explained as the visitor strode inside. 'He's come to apologise, start again, on a better footing.' He raised his eyebrows at Hilton, just a fraction. His uncle was no fool, Hilton knew.

'I wondered if you might have a little of that Blaze's Best for me to try,' Huxley smiled, in a very friendly way. 'Old man Morrison told me about it. Seems it's an important part of your success.'

Uncle Norbert sent Hilton up to the bedroom where the sacks of food were still standing. He was armed with a carrier bag. Hilton ladled out half a bagful as he cast his mind back to that strange day at Bingley's. Perhaps the food was the special ingredient in their new-found success, he thought. Maybe the shower of glitter was just coincidence.

From the bedroom window, he looked down the narrow lane to see a very flash, yellow car parked on the road at the end. It looked like it belonged to Huxley. Everything he owned seemed to be oversized and he obviously liked yellow.

The carrier bag tugged on Hilton's arm. That was more than enough for the nasty piece of work. As he took the peace offering back through to the kitchen, his Uncle Norbert and Horace Huxley were stirring cups of tea, and oddly, starting to sound like pals.

It was all a little worrying, but Hilton knew his uncle was no idiot. He'd not be taken in by this proposal of joint success now they were doing very well on their own.

'Past your bedtime, lad,' Uncle Norbert said, tapping the cracked face on his wristwatch. After he'd politely said goodnight, Hilton closed the kitchen door behind him and made his way upstairs. The one thing Hilton didn't do was go to bed.

Instead, he sat at the top of the stairs and listened. To be sure.

After he had heard for the fifth time the story of little Lottie who had escaped and taken up with a weasel in Hopewell Woods,

Hilton decided everything was going to be alright. Ferret peace had broken out. He was looking forward to hearing more about Huxley's visit when he woke next morning, and he went to sleep feeling happy.

SETTLED IN HIS NOCTURNAL HABITAT, Hilton burrowed into the most brilliant dream.

He lifted each cup everyone had been talking about at the National Championships as Bagley Festival came to a close. Ferrets from across the country came to compete with those from the East Northumbria Ferret Boarding and Welfare Society, but the winners all came from one place, Uncle Norbert's sheds. Their animal housing was transformed into a brand-new swanky modern ferret village, with posh buildings where the creatures lived, pens that cleaned automatically, a piped-in water supply, and feeders filled from a stock in the roof space which flowed down as they emptied. There was a special bathhouse with a built-in pool and gentle driers that wouldn't overheat the jills and hobs, and of course, hammocks, hundreds of them, in different colours, so every creature could have their turn. There was nothing for Hilton and his uncle to do except play with the healthy, bright-eyed, curious animals they were so proud of.

But when Hilton woke up next morning, things were not like that at all.

Chapter Seventeen – The Yellow Car Vanishes

'UNCLE, I'VE HAD A most brilliant dream,' he started, desperate to share how they could develop the sheds once they won more prize money. He pushed opened the kitchen door and got a bad feeling at what he saw.

Cups littered the table, and the remains of the tea, strong and brown, clung in dark rings to the insides. Huxley must've been here for some time, he thought.

Casting his eyes around, he noticed a broken mug on the floor. Its sharp white shards were scattered across the red tiles. As he opened his mouth to call for the old man, something caught his eye. The back door had been left open. Just slightly, in a not-completely-closed kind of way. He pulled at it.

'Uncle Norbert, where are you?' he called, feeling worried. He wondered if he might still be in bed, having the same sort of wonderful ferret dream as him. Hilton ran upstairs and peeked into the old man's bedroom. It was empty. The blankets covering the bare mattress had not been touched.

Was Uncle Norbert up and sorting out in the sheds already, he wondered? He ran downstairs and pulled open the back door. There was nothing odd to be seen, but his uncle wasn't there either.

'Uncle Norbert, you busy?' he called, making his way across to Bluebell Lodge where they started each morning. He was beginning to get a bit of a knot, the same one that would twist in his stomach when his mum or dad needed to 'speak' to him.

But his uncle was not silly, he kept telling himself.

As he approached the first shed, he could see immediately that the door hadn't been closed properly in the way his uncle usually left it. Things sounded unusually quiet inside, no scurrying and scampering of the animals hungry for their first feed of the day. As he pulled the door open, Hilton could see something was wrong. There were less animals than yesterday.

Had there been a break-out? He scanned around and counted. Rodders? Yes, he was there. Neville? Scurrying around the pen, a little faster than usual.

Ogden…where was Ogden? Hilton peered into the sleeping area. It was empty. Ogden was missing.

He quickly checked the jills' side of the pen. Rubina had gone too. The ferrets that won their festival events, Ogden for his agility, and Rubina for her speed, both vanished.

That couldn't be bad luck, or an escape. And still no sign of Uncle Norbert.

Leaving the ferrets behind, he turned to look down the long lane, where the bushes and shrubs leaned breezily into the narrow track. The yellow car parked on the road last night had gone.

What was happening at the East Northumbria Ferret Boarding and Welfare Society?

Chapter Eighteen – Calling for Back-Up

THERE WAS ONLY ONE REASON for stealing a prize-winning hob and jill together, Hilton concluded, as he did his uncle's funny whistley thing. But, where was Uncle Norbert? Hilton was lost for ideas.

Rodders was propped against the mesh divider, his paws resting on the wire, staring with his one brown eye and one red, straight at the boy. Not blinking but looking directly at him.

Hilton was thinking. He would need help, he decided. Time to ring his mum and dad. They would be cross that Norbert had wandered off leaving their ten-year-old alone, but everyone knew there would be a good reason.

'Back soon, Rodders,' he said.

He made his way toward the house and picked up the old cream handset of the only telephone Uncle Norbert possessed, the one attached to the wall by a long, grey flex. Usually, there was a long burrrrrrrr sound that stopped when Hilton pressed the numbers of his mum's mobile phone, then what followed was the ring-ring, ring-ring, until she answered.

He tried those things. There was nothing. No burrrrrrrr, no ring-ring. Just silence. He put back the handset.

Hilton couldn't recall the last time he cried, but he remembered the same tightness in his chest, the prickling feeling in the corners of his eyes, and that sensation of a hand around his throat, making it difficult to breathe.

What he needed right now was to feel the warm soft fur or hear the happy squeak of his only pal. Rodders.

He closed the back door and went back to Bluebell Lodge. The air would be sweet to breathe, and the ferrety noises make him feel better.

But he was not ready for what greeted him there.

Chapter Nineteen – It's All in a Name

'WHAT TOOK *YOU* SO LONG?'

Hilton couldn't work out where the voice was coming from as he stepped back inside the shed. 'Huh?' was all he could say.

'Over here!'

Hilton's keen ears followed the sound. He tracked with his eyes too, scanning the enclosures to find himself staring into one brown eye, and one red. Rodders' head was tilted to one side as he stood, still propped at the divider.

Hilton stared at the cheeky masked face, unable to believe what he was seeing or hearing.

'Thought you'd work it out a faster, being a Ferret Boy,' Rodders went on.

'Work out what?'

'The Ferret Master vanishing with Ogden and Rubina.'

'You know what happened to them?'

'Watched it all,' Rodders continued. 'We were asleep when the Ferret Fiend came in. Had a scout around 'til he found who he was looking for. Put them into his travelling ferret house.'

'And Uncle Norbert? Where's he, then?'

'Didn't see the Ferret Master, but I'd guess he's wherever Ogden and Rubina are.'

'Was it Huxley, the …Ferret Fiend, the… man, I mean, who took them?'

'We were too frightened to look at his face, but he sounded like the one who stole my granddaddy from The Ferret Master.'

'You know this?' Hilton asked.

'Since the Ferret Mistress left, we don't go out often. But when we visit the festivals, there is talk. Everyone says my granddaddy was kidnapped, swapped for a loser when they were at Bagley Festival. My daddy, Rodders the second, told me when I was a kit.'

'A kid?' Hilton said, confused.

'A kit, a baby ferret! *You'll* never make a Ferret Master, and we had high hopes for you.'

'Where should I start?' Hilton asked.

'You should start by taking me. Not much use on your own.'

HILTON TOOK RODDERS FROM HIS pen and draped him like a furry scarf around his shoulders. 'Stay there, whilst I think,' he said, feeling quite stuck.

What did he know? Where could he start? He knew Huxley's name and would recognise his twisted, scary face. Huxley could have taken his uncle and ferret friends anywhere.

Hilton might never see them again.

The boy sat at the kitchen table, putting the ferret down on its surface. Rodders scurried across the worktop to where the old telephone rested, along with a messy pile of Norbert's business papers.

'Please don't chew the cable,' the boy warned. 'I'm in enough trouble,' but Rodders continued to sniff at the books and papers until something made his whiskers tweak. At the very bottom of the mess were bills and important-looking letters escaping from a box marked, 'Urgent'.

'*This one!*' he squeaked, resting his paw on a thick, yellow, boring-looking book with no pictures, a soft back and only words and numbers on the cover. It was brown at the edges and the corners of the pages were splayed where they had been flicked and turned over many, many times.

'How's *this* going to help?' Hilton puffed.

'The Ferret Master used it all the time. When he wanted our special food, he pulled it out. Or when we were short of bedding. There might be something inside,' the little voice explained.

Hilton pulled out the weighty book and read the front cover. 'East Northumbria Telephone Business Directory,' he said. 'Ah, Huxley might be listed here, or maybe, where he lives?'

He flicked through the alphabetical section of the directory. 'H…H…Hall….Seed Merchant, nope. Hunwick Happy Rabbit Home. We're getting closer. Here it is!' He pointed at the information and looked at his ferret friend.

'Reading's not my strong point, Ferret Boy,' Rodders sniffed.

'Huxley's,' Hilton read aloud. 'Northumbria's Number One for Ferrets. *That's him*! Spine Acre Farm, Dalworthy. Now we know where to start, Rodders!'

Chapter Twenty – The Perfect Plan

'WE'LL NEED REINFORCEMENTS,' Rodders said. 'You're not the *strongest* Ferret Boy, after all.'

Hilton paused. The four-legged furry scarf was right. Would two of them be enough to find and overcome Huxley? To save Uncle Norbert and his prize-winning ferrets?

'What's your thinking, Ferret Boy?' Rodders asked.

'Well, what I'm thinking, what I'm actually wondering, is… how you are… that erm, *you're* talking! Since when?' Hilton asked, his eyebrows knitting together in a puzzled expression.

'No need to speak when the Ferret Master's here,' Rodders continued. 'He does everything we need.'

'Makes sense,' Hilton said, nodding his head. 'I need to get something first.'

In the prize money envelope collected at the festival, a few coins rattled around in the corners. Hilton thought about his bus fare from home to school on days when dad had the car. And Dalworthy was a little further, so he took out a one pound and a two-pound coin. He bit his lip slightly. It felt mean dipping into his uncle's first winnings for a long time. He wondered whether this would ever get everyone back to safety, but he had to try.

His only help was a handful of ferrets. 'Who shall we take, Rodders? Your call.'

At the door to Bluebell Lodge, Rodders called out. 'Attenshun! Our Ferret Master's missing, with Ogden and Rubina. We need your help!'

Each ferret scampered from their sleeping quarters and gathered at the wire divider. They waited quietly in line.

'Mabel...we need your maze-solving skills. Neville, those whiskers can find anything. And, who are our biggest, strongest? Jagger...Winifred. Open the pens, Ferret Boy.'

'You promise ...promise not to run off?' Hilton asked. Escaped animals would make things a whole lot worse.

Rodders gave a sniff. 'We'd be *mad* to run away from *our* Ferret Master, but, if we had *Huxley*.... Hurry, now, what's the plan?'

'There's a bus stop at the end of the lane. All services go through Dalworthy. But I've no idea where Spine Acre Farm is,' Hilton said, scratching his head. 'And I'm not sure I like the sound of it.'

'Let's start with that. When we reach Dalworthy, we can ferret about,' Rodders squeaked. Watching the creatures from of the corners of his eyes, just in case, Hilton closed the back door. In the porch lay the carrier used for the trip to Bingley's and the festival.

'That's it!' he said. 'Rodders, I need *you* with me. And another small one, maybe you, Mabel?'

He looked at who he'd chosen to travel together.

'Jump in both of you and mind your manners. The rest, you stick close by. I'll tell you what to do when the bus comes.'

IT WAS A BEAUTIFUL DAY. The sun was shining and the heat was building. Hilton's head felt close to bursting as he dodged the greenery down the lane, armed with two coins in his pocket, a pair of ferrets in a carrier, and three loose at his side.

This was not a good start.

Chapter Twenty-One – An Important Operation

HILTON LOOKED AT THE BUS stop. Crossing with his uncaged ferrety friends was a worry, but they needed to reach the brick shelter with weeds growing through its cracks in order to hide. Neville, Winifred and Jagger paused patiently, waiting for Hilton's signal.

'After three,' he said, 'and stick close by.'

Hilton chose the longest gap between the few cars on the quiet road and set off for the other side. The ferrets tracked his steps and stayed near him as they reached the cool shade of the stop. They huddled together in its darkest corner.

Hilton put down the carrier.

'This is how it'll work,' he said. 'There's no way they'll let me on the bus with you lot. When it arrives, the three of you stay in the shade and climb beneath when the driver's taking my fare. You're good at getting into little holes. Find a safe space to stow away and hang on. It's not far, but it's bumpy in places. Each time the bus makes a stop, watch for my shoes stepping down. When *it is* me, jump off as quickly as you can.'

'Like stowaways?' Jagger asked.

'Oh man!' Mabel said. 'I love being a Secret Squirrel.'

'I fixed a squirrel once,' Hilton recalled. 'I'll tell you the story when we're back safely.' If that ever happens, he thought.

As the bus approached the stop, the three loose ferrets squished themselves into the dark, dank corner of the brick walls. Hilton stepped forward, the cage facing the wrong direction so the driver couldn't see inside.

'Dalworthy, please,' he asked, as nicely as he could.

'One pound, young man,' the driver said, as the white ticket spilled out of the machine. 'Poorly puss?' He nodded his head in the direction of the carrier.

Hilton smiled back at the man and took his ticket. Walking down the bus, he imagined the trio finding ferret-sized spaces underneath, inside the engine compartment or the wheel arches, to complete their journey. He passed a man sitting on the front seat, with a sandy coloured terrier. The dog strained on its lead and sniffed the air, growling at the carrier as Hilton passed.

The boy took a deep breath and swallowed hard.

'Now, now. You'll frighten the cat, Alfie,' the man apologised, poking at toffee stuck in his front teeth from a bag in his other hand. His bright red hair stuck out from beneath a checked cap.

Common red fox, Vulpes vulpes, p17. Live in parks and woodland edges and will readily eat whatever is available (including toffee). *Red foxes* (and their pets) *have excellent hearing. They can hear low-frequency sounds and rodents digging underground* (and possibly under buses).

Hilton chose the last empty seat and sat down carefully, positioning the cage door out of view. Six stops, that's all. Six stops. Count, and stay calm, Hilton, he thought.

Chapter Twenty – Two- Steamed Up

THE CAGE FITTED NICELY ONTO Hilton's knee and he began to relax a little as the bus picked up speed. He crossed his fingers and hoped the little animals were hanging on below and would come to no harm. He'd seen Mabel clamber expertly through the maze, and Rubina could run. They were skilful little critters, he told himself.

The sun shone brightly through the window and Hilton could feel its heat on his arm. He was starting to feel a little warm, the plastic carrier holding the heat close in his lap, while he was deciding his plan for once they left the bus.

Alfie the terrier kept straining on his lead and staring at the cat carrier. Alfie knew how cats smelled and whatever was in that cage, it was not a cat, he was sure. He pulled and growled as his owner tugged at the red lead, tutting and calling the dog under his breath for being disobedient.

'*You'd* never win at Crufts, son,' he said, as he yanked back the dog which had scrabbled its way a little closer to Hilton and the cage. 'I should've stuck with a Jack Russell. My poor Timmy could always follow commands.'

The dog's wet blackberry nose sniffed in an offended way, its head up in the air, eyes still locked firmly on the carrier containing Rodders and Mabel. He pulled harder on the lead as his long pink tongue lolled from the side of his mouth, showing a very full set of sharp white teeth.

'You're getting over-excited, son. It's just a cat,' the man said. 'You've seen them before.' He shook his head at Hilton, who was trying hard to ignore what the dog was doing.

Beads of sweat began to pop on Hilton's brow and he watched Alfie very closely, afraid that if the dog pulled away from his owner, the carrier full of ferrets might be found out.

They had travelled a short way when Hilton noticed a hissing sound. The driver was making muttering noises to himself at the front of the bus. 'Not now, lass. Not now,' he kept saying, leaning over his dashboard and tutting.

The bus pulled slowly to the side of the road and came to a halt where there was no bus stop, no houses, and no other traffic.

The driver turned to the passengers and wiped his brow. 'She's overheating,' he said, shrugging his shoulders. The man with the terrier sighed loudly. 'Let her cool off a few minutes and we'll be back on our way, mate,' he explained, pulling down the sun visor as he got back into his seat. 'Sit tight, folks. Not be long.'

Hilton's stare remained fixed on Alfie the beady, brown-eyed terrier, who twinkled a wicked glare, waiting to tug forward and taste his first ferret sandwich. The dog's lead was tight in his owner's hand, which was red and puffy and extended towards the middle of the bus.

'I hope he's not frightening your moggy, son,' he smiled. 'He's not usually like this.'

Hilton's back was sticking to the bus seat and he needed to take off his coat. He could feel his face turn a deeper shade of pink and blew out a long hot breath as everyone on the bus shuffled in the rising temperature. His left foot began to cramp. He knew that awful, knotted feeling, and he could hear what his mum would say if she were next to him right now: 'Stretch it out, it's the only way.'

Hilton pushed his toes forward and felt the oddest sensation, his shoe taking on a life of its own and pulling away from his foot.

He looked down. There, with his teeth firmly embedded in Hilton's shoe was Jagger, tugging with all his might to get Hilton's attention. The boy scanned around the bus quickly. He needed to know what Alfie was doing. The dog was quiet, stroked by his owner.

Hilton looked down and whispered. '*You're* meant to be under the bus!'

Jagger spat out Hilton shoe. 'Why the wait?' he said. 'We thought you'd got off…I found a hole to come check.'

'Well, go back,' Hilton said, waggling his foot to help Jagger on his way. 'We'll set off again in a minute. Stick to the plan.'

'You speaking to me, son?' the dog's owner said, turning to Hilton.

'I was talking to my cat, sorry,' the boy mumbled, gently nudging the nosy ferret on the floor back into the hole he'd emerged from. He patted the carrier as he looked out of the window.

'There we go!' the bus driver said, as the engine started once more with no sign of the horrible hissing noise. At last, they were on their way again.

Chapter Twenty-Three – The Potato Woman

AT THE NEXT STOP, THE man with the terrier got off, and Hilton smiled as he passed outside the bus. The dog barked loudly, sniffing, and pulling the man back towards it.

'What's got into *you*, today, Alfie?' he heard the man say, tugging the dog away from the bus in a bad-tempered way as his checked cap fell off his head and landed on the ground. Hilton knew why the dog was barking and hoped it hadn't frightened the stowaways.

NO-ONE WAS WAITING AT the next stop. Or the one after that. At stop number four, Cawston Road Ends, a woman almost fell onto the bus with four heavy bags of shopping. In the scuffle to get on, her potatoes broke loose from their plastic bag and rolled off in different directions, one along the aisle, another travelling under the front seat. She tutted loudly, but the bus driver waited patiently until her potatoes were under control before setting off. She plumped down loudly on the seat in front of Hilton as he bent down to retrieve a rogue potato which had landed at his feet.

'I think this is yours,' he said, offering it to her and smiling his best genuine smile.

As she turned to take back her knobbly brown vegetable, she stared at the carrier on Hilton's knee.

'What you got in there?' she asked, twisting her head to focus her beady amber eyes on the cage. Hilton imagined a long, black forked tongue flicking from her mouth to help identify its contents.

Vipera berus, the common adder, page 5. Most commonly seen during sunset, when they go out to hunt (this one's body clock is all wrong*). Their venom is not highly lethal but could still be fatal, mostly for children or the elderly* (best avoided, then). *Humans are most likely to be bitten if they step on or try to pick up an adder.*

'I'm off to the vets,' he explained. Hilton tried to widen his smile, but she would not be distracted.

'Doesn't look like a cat from here,' she hissed crossly, looking down into the air holes on top of the cage. 'And there's two of them. *They're rats*!' Her tongue, very visible as she complained, was pink, not black, he noted, and no sign of a fork.

Other passengers looked round and started to fidget. 'We're nearly there now,' Hilton replied, patting the top. 'Five more minutes.' Please hurry up, please hurry up, he thought.

'Rats aren't allowed on public transport!' she continued. 'They're disgusting. Driver! This lad's got a cage full of rats.'

A deep voice came from the front of the bus. 'As long as they're in a cage, missus, he can bring on what he likes…'

Take that, missus, Hilton thought. Sometimes, what you need is a big old kick from a bus-driver-wallaby to shut down the conversation.

Bennetts wallaby, Macropus rufogriseus, page 49. Although an undeniable fact that the wallaby is not native to the British Isles, that has not stopped imported colonies from flourishing in the wild. For example, a colony of more than 100 can be found on the Isle of Man having originally bred from a single pair that escaped from a nearby wildlife park some years ago.

The woman tutted. 'Ridiculous!' she huffed.

'…I'd like it to be a crocodile myself,' the driver added, under his breath.

Hilton was relieved as the bus approached Dalworthy. The potato woman kept looking round and pulling faces, but the driver just shook his head. Hilton pressed the bell for the bus to stop and walked to the front, making sure the cage didn't swing too much, frightening Rodders and Mabel. Something inside him was tied in a knot. It was getting tighter by the minute.

'Good luck with your crocodile, lad,' the bus driver winked, as Hilton stepped off. He slowly circled his foot in mid-air between the bus and the kerb, giving the ferrets as much signal to squiggle out of their hiding holes as he could.

As the bus chugged off along the quiet country road, the three ferrets circled Hilton's legs. They were grubby and gave little squeaky coughs.

'All present and correct,' said Rodders from inside the carrier. 'Let's get our Ferret Master back!'

Chapter Twenty-Four – Finding Spine Acre

'DALWORTHY'S NOT A HUGE PLACE,' Hilton said, as he gathered the animals together, away from the roadside. 'We'll just have to look around. Spine Acre Farm...sounds horrible.'

'This is where we need Neville,' Rodders reminded him. 'He can sniff out other ferrets in an instant.'

The six set out along a lane, narrow and muddy, and in a short while, they saw a sign. HESKETH HOUSE FARM, it read.

Hilton told the Ferret Five to stay where they were. He was going to ask for directions to Spine Acre Farm, and before long, he returned.

'It's the next opening down here,' he said, 'but the farmer asked why I'd need to go *there*. Not many visitors, apparently.'

As they hurried down the lane, Neville's whiskers tweaked and his pace quickened until he was running, his body bobbing up and down like a furry carriage on a country rollercoaster.

'He's onto something,' Rodders said. 'Let's follow!'

They caught up with him at a pair of tall stone pillars. A gated driveway bore a big black sign. SPINE ACRE FARM. NO ENTRY.

Below, it read, HUXLEY'S, NORTHUMBRIA'S NUMBER ONE FOR FERRETS.

Hilton looked along the driveway. At the end was an even taller gate, and just beyond, the same big, yellow car as when Huxley visited last night. 'That's his. We're in the right place.'

The six walked up the long driveway, stopping at the gate. It was much higher than Hilton. He scratched his head, wondering how to get over. If he'd been allowed to climb that fence at school, he'd have known exactly how to tackle it.

Through the fancy black ironwork, he saw faces he recognised. Jagger, Winifred and Neville peered at him from the other side!

'Ferrets-one, Ferret Boy-nil,' Rodders said, from inside the cage.

'Okay then, here we go.' Hilton put one foot up into the scrolls of the metal gate ready to climb. He reached high and pulled himself up, but the cage swung violently in his other hand.

'Hey, Ferret Boy! *You'll* kill us before we get there.'

Hilton stepped back down. 'I don't know what to do,' he said. 'Suppose I could leave you here, on this side of the gate 'til we get back.'

'You've a *lot* to learn…' Rodders tutted. 'Let us out and throw the carrier over. You climb. We'll meet you on the other side.'

Chapter Twenty-Five – Number One for Ferrets

THE OTHER SIDE LOOKED VERY unwelcoming. Large black metal sheds formed neat rows with gravel walkways between. The shed doors were locked by long metal bars slotted across the fronts. Big red signs warned visitors: KEEP OUT.

The Ferret Five were silent.

'My whiskers are picking up bad vibes,' Neville said. 'We need to find the Ferret Master quickly. This place is making my fur stand on end.' Mabel's bottom lip gave a little ferret quiver.

'Is anyone in there?' Hilton said, knocking quietly on the dark front door as the creatures began to move oddly, in circles, twirling and darting in and out of one another. 'And, what *is* wrong with you lot?'

'Can't you hear?' Jagger asked. 'There's lots in there. We've got to go in.'

'Lots of what? I can't hear a thing.'

'Need your bat-hearing, Ferret Boy. It's where Huxley keeps his creatures, and they don't sound very happy.'

'We'll never get inside,' Hilton said. 'His security's too good.'

Mabel appeared from round a corner. 'I've scouted round the back,' she said. 'We might have more luck round there.'

Together, the gang sized up the metal building. There was no back door, no window. No way of getting in. Hilton bent down to examine a small, slatted opening near the base of the shed.

'If my memory serves me right, this is an outside vent, a fan of some sort....' he said, poking the white plastic shutter, and then grabbing it with both hands. 'Don't stand there watching. Help me to pull it off!'

Jagger, the strongest hob, sunk his teeth into Hilton's coat, and pulled backwards while the others watched. 'Join in...all of you!' Hilton said, as the creatures scuttled around the Ferret Boy's coat and yanked with all their ferret strength. 'It's like The Enormous Turnip! One last effort, you lot!' the boy shouted, as the cover came off in his hands, leaving him to roll onto the gravel path.

'You'll never get through there, Ferret Boy,' Neville said. 'It's far too small.'

'It's a good size for you,' Hilton said, nodding towards the open gap in the shed. 'Check it out, but don't be long. We've still not found Uncle Norbert and the others yet. We need to get a wriggle on.'

'Getting a wriggle on, that's our job. Very funny, Ferret Boy.'

THE FERRET FIVE POPPED BACK out of the hole one by one. They were silent, their usually happy heads down. 'It's just too awful,' Mabel sniffed.

'I'd never swap their sheds for ours,' Neville said. 'And they've automatic feeders, automatic water and bedding dispensers...Nothing is done by a human. No friendly hands.'

'Really?' Hilton asked, on his knees, peering into the hole, where all he could see was darkness.

'Tell the Ferret Boy what they said about their keeper. Grim listening.'

Rodders shook his little furry head. 'Their Ferret Master doesn't even *like* ferrets. Never touches them or talks to them. They go from cages, to shows, to cages and back here again. All they have is each other, and each week, some leave the shed and never return.'

The gang nodded at one another.

'Uncle Norbert would never treat you like that,' Hilton said. 'He loves you more than anything in the world. And, speaking of Uncle Norbert, we've not located him yet.'

Mabel tugged at the hem of Hilton's trousers. 'Can we come back later and help them, Hilton? This is not good. Not good at all.'

Jagger interrupted. 'Let's get our Ferret Master back first! And, Ogden and Rubina, here we come!'

'Yes, yes, Mabel. I promise, once we've found the Ferret Master, I mean, Uncle Norbert.'

'We'll be back!' Mabel squeaked down through the dark chasm as her friends ran off to find their Master and missing pals.

Chapter Twenty-Six – A Shaft of Sunlight

'THIS LOOKS A POSSIBILITY.'

Hilton was looking at an old barn made of unpainted and warped boards, with doors that didn't quite meet in the middle. All around, the farm was silent except for occasional cow or sheep noise somewhere off in the beautiful green distance. The building looked abandoned and unused. Rooftiles had crashed to the ground from the holey roof above, creating piles of red powdery dust and broken tile fragments. Tall weeds grew around its base, like a pretty frame, their yellow heads in full bloom, facing the early afternoon sunshine.

'What do you think, Rodders?' Hilton said.

'Can't think for hunger. We've not been fed today, Ferret Boy.'

Neville's long whiskers flicked excitedly. 'That's a sure sign there's food inside,' Rodders said. 'Let's check.'

Hilton put down the empty cage and pushed the door slightly. It creaked open. A shaft of sunlight streamed inside. Slowly letting their eyes adjust to the gloomy darkness, they stepped in.

'Hmm…smells like….Blaze's Best if I'm not mistaken,' Neville said.

The sun illuminated the inside of the barn, its strong rays scudding across the dusty floor, highlighting every particle of the dancing dirt that swirled within. 'I just can't quite….see. Oh, Blaze's Best. Neville, you were right.'

Stacked against the furthest wall of the barn were sacks, too many to count, of the same feed bought at Bingley's a couple of weeks ago. Row upon row, standing propped against one another, each with that white ferret and the Blaze name proudly displayed.

Hilton heard a sound. It was faint but coming from deep in the shadows. He strained his bat-ears and stood still, scanning around in the gloom. Time to turn on owl vision.

Barn owl, Tyto alba, page 9, unable to clearly see anything within a few inches of their eyes. However, their far vision – particularly in low light conditions – is incredibly good.

'Shhh, you lot,' he said, looking down at the Ferret Five scuttling around on the dirty floor. 'Where's that noise coming from?' Suddenly a hay bale moved a little, then again. He homed in closer. Hilton watched as strands fluttered from it down to the ground. The bale rocked slightly.

The boy checked behind to find his uncle, gagged, and tied up on the floor. He was covered in dust, his hands bound by a rough rope full of large knots. One side of a pair of handcuffs was attached to a cattle feeder and stopped him shuffling far. A handkerchief filled his mouth and his eyes were wide.

'Uncle Norbert! What happened?'

The old man took a huge gulp of air as the gag was pulled from his mouth. He recounted how Huxley had bundled him from the house and forced him down the lane where he was pushed into the boot of the car. Ogden and Rubina had travelled in a carrier, belted carefully onto the front seat.

'He said there was only room for one passenger!' Uncle Norbert said, hopelessly offended. He had been in Huxley's barn, tied up, all night.

'He's bought *all* the Blaze's Best in the north east, Hilton. He says with that, and his two new ferrets, Ogden and Rubina, he's going to sweep the board at the National Championships in September. He's gone completely mad!'

'We need to get you untied, Uncle,' Hilton said.

As he leaned forward to pull at the knots behind the old man's back, the ferrets disappeared, darting away leaving Hilton alone. They vanished into the straw bales and were nowhere to be seen. Each and every one.

'Hey! What the…?'

An explosion of light flooded the barn as the door was flung open. Framed in the open doorway, the spikey silhouette of Huxley, tall and thin and with dark, wild hair.

Chapter Twenty-Seven – A Ferret-Stealing Fraudster

'COME EQUIPPED TO STEAL BACK your prize-winners?' Huxley sneered as he kicked the discarded carrier through the air like a football. It landed with a clatter at Hilton's feet.

The boy's heart was beating inside his ears, louder and stronger than ever before. There was no way out. He was beaten now.

His uncle was tied up, and Hilton couldn't release him. His five helpers had taken fright and run away. And, this tall ferret-stealing fraudster was terrifying...

'You see, son,' Huxley hissed, 'there's only room for one Number One in Northumbria, and that's *me*. Thought you were doing well, eh? Well, I know your secret and you won't get Blaze's Best within a hundred miles. And with your little winners, over there....'

He pointed out his super-cage in a dusty corner of the barn, where Ogden and Rubina were scuttling around inside sounding very unhappy.

'*Shut up!* he yelled at them. 'You'll be winning the Grand National and The Maze for me soon enough! So you, lad, will be keeping *this* old fool company 'til then. I'll make sure *you* can't enter. I'll tell the police I caught you breaking into *my* barn, stealing *my* animals. I'll say that's how *you* became successful again. You'll both go to prison!'

He threw his head back and laughed as he pulled out another piece of rope and grabbed Hilton by the shoulders.

'The best thing about Spine Acre,' he said, tying the boy at his ankles and wrists, 'is that *no one* will hear you!' From his trouser pocket, he pulled the key to the handcuffs and swapped one bracelet onto Hilton, slotting it back through the cattle feeder, binding the uncle and nephew together in that spot, forever.

There was no escape.

Huxley tugged at the chain. 'That's going nowhere,' he said. 'Just in case you were *thinking* of making a run for it.' He walked towards the brilliant sunshine outside, kicking the door shut behind him.

Hilton and his uncle were in almost total darkness. A single shaft of light wangled through the gap between the rotten doors.

Chapter Twenty-Eight – Waiting for the Worst to Happen

Hilton and his uncle were attached, inescapably so. He could feel the warmth of the old man's body and manage just the tiniest of shuffles. The darkness hid Hilton's tears, and he listened to his Uncle Norbert's breath. In and out through his nose, slowly and deliberately, like everything else the old man did.

This was it.

The captive pair were completely alone. No-one would suspect Huxley. Even the Ferret Five had scurried off when the beast of Spine Acre Farm made his appearance at the barn door.

The phone wasn't working at Uncle Norbert's and his mum and dad would think everything was fine until the weekly phone call didn't happen. And then what? When no-one answered, they'd keep trying.

Then, they'd get cross, hare-box, and agree they probably shouldn't have left Hilton there after all. They'd drive out to the East Northumbria Ferret Boarding and Welfare Society, only to find no-one there.

They'd assume the pair were off buying ferret food when they couldn't be found amongst the sheds. They'd make a cup of tea, have another argument, and wait. When Hilton and his uncle didn't return at teatime, his mum and dad would call the police. The police would come, look round, take details.

How would they know where to start looking for the boy and his uncle? Would anyone else realise that ferrets had vanished? Probably not.

How long would the whole thing take? There was simply nothing to do but wait. And breathe. Slowly. Through his nose.

He wondered how he'd got here. Wished he'd been a more sensible person, maybe not flicked his shoe over the fence or put the apple into the urinal as a joke. Maybe that way, his mum and dad would've been happier with him.

Prouder of what he'd achieved. At school. In life. Maybe he'd be spending the summer with them, not sent to stay with his uncle. All he'd succeeded at so far was to mend an injured squirrel. Hardly something to boast about.

Except for his Best Junior Handler award, of course. Which his parents didn't know about yet. And might never find out. If they were incredibly lucky, that might happen in some future phone call. But that wouldn't be happening any time soon.

If…

at…

all.

In the dark, Uncle Norbert nudged Hilton's leg, once, twice, three times. Hilton nudged back. It felt good to be in touch. He liked being close to his uncle. It made him feel a little safer, that he wasn't alone. This would have to do.

In the suffocating darkness of the barn, all Hilton could do was listen. And organise his breathing, very carefully.

Off in the far distance, he could hear a tractor, probably working on Hesketh Hall farm, he thought. Birds were singing, and the leaves on the trees rustled in the warm summer breeze. Then, there was a noise.

A scuttle, at first. Then little feet, scampering. A rat, Hilton thought. This was definitely the kind of place a rat would feel at home.

Brown rats, Rattus norvegicus, page 16, usually prefer ground living and burrowing, can be known to climb (great for that in here). *Preferred food is cereals* (like Blaze's Best) *although they are omnivorous.*

Then, came a sniff. And another, followed by more scuffling. Something was moving around on the floor next to him. Hilton's body tensed as he waited for the bite about to come. He tightened everything in his face and pulled his limbs in close.

Chapter Twenty-Nine – A Top Team

HILTON'S MUSCLES WERE RIGID. HE braced himself for pain. A sharp nip. But the sniffing and the scampering continued. Something climbed onto his legs. He could feel immediately it was too long, much too long, to be a rat or a mouse.

'Let's get to work,' a ferrety squeak pronounced.

'Jagger, get up and pull out their gags, let them breathe. Then, work with Winifred to get through the ropes. They're thick, but you can do it. Mabel, were you watching where Huxley put that key?' Rodders asked.

'I saw,' she said. 'It's in his car.'

'Then use that flexi body of yours to get in from underneath, like we did on the bus. Neville, check on Ogden and Rubina. They're awfully quiet.'

Hilton could hear movement across the barn. Scampers and scurries were followed by a strange feeling of tugging at the ropes that bound him, gnawing sharp teeth biting into the knots at his wrists, while little legs climbed upon him, and reached up towards his face.

'Need your help, Ferret Boy,' Jagger said, his front paws resting on Hilton's chest as the furry friend looked up towards the boy's mouth. 'Open a little wider. This went in. It *has* to come out.'

Between his teeth, Jagger nipped the loose end of the hankie and threw his body into reverse. As he pulled, back, back, back, his sinewy leg muscles strained, every fibre of his fuzzy being working to help his friend.

Inside Hilton's mouth, the bulk of fabric started to vanish like a magic trick. He wiggled his jaw as if he'd just been to the dentist. Come on boy... you can do it, he wanted to say, as the creature continued, tugging his hardest.

Suddenly, Jagger tumbled back, somersaulting uncontrollably across the floor as the material spewed from Hilton's mouth and he could speak again. 'Such a relief,' he said. 'That chewing thing tickles though.'

Before long, Uncle Norbert's gag was out too. 'You're doing a grand job there, Winifred,' Norbert said, as the ropes binding his ankles fell apart, leaving messy fibres in bundles on the floor. 'Ogden and Rubina look fine,' he whispered, 'but they'll be better when we're all out of here.'

'Only the handcuffs now. Where's Mabel?' Hilton asked, peering through the darkness, the barn door still firmly closed. From the other side came the sound of little paws sprinting across the dusty floor. Mabel's dainty ferret feet.

There was a faint metallic tinkle as something was dropped. 'How did you manage that, you genius?' Mabel stood over the key and looked directly into Hilton's eyes. Then at Uncle Norbert. And back to Hilton.

Hilton was puzzled. 'Why isn't she talking, Uncle?' he asked.

'She's a ferret, daft lad!'

Of course she didn't speak, Hilton thought. The Ferret Master was back in control.

She nudged the key close to Norbert's free hand, and his fingers scrabbled a little in the dirt to match up the key and keyhole in the dark. 'That's it, lad. We're out of here!'

A single ray of early evening sunlight squeezed through the badly fitting doors. 'Put Ogden and Rubina into *our* carrier,' the old man whispered as they edged towards the rickety barn door. 'I won't let that crook say we've stolen a single thing, not even a ferret cage.'

'What are we going to do, Uncle?'

'Get out of here and hide 'til it's dark. It'll be safer to make our way home then.'

'Will we have to walk all the way?'

'What else are we going to do, boy? Steal Huxley's car?'

Closing the barn door behind them, the nine skulked around the back of the building. They sidled along rotting walls, and crept carefully through the farm, Jagger keeping look-out as they moved stealthily and silently, one by one. They edged past the sheds and down the side of the tall hedge until they found a gap in the wall that entombed the horrid Spine Acre Farm.

At last, they were free.

Chapter Thirty – The Promise

THEY WERE HUDDLING TOGETHER WHERE the wall had collapsed into a pile of bricks, the seven ferrets, uncle and boy, when a jill's ferrety voice prodded the inside of Hilton's head. 'You *promised*, Hilton. You said we'd go back.'

Hilton shook his head, trying to release those words, set them free out into the open air, make them nothing to do with him now they had completed their mission. They were ready to go home.

'You *promised*.'

The words poked inside Hilton's brain like sharp needles. Now, he had a different problem; another mission that wasn't really his. However…

Mabel had won the Maze. Rubina had aced the Grand National. Would the Best Junior Handler walk away? Break a Ferret Promise? Hadn't the furry bendy buses given Hilton such fun? Been loyal to him and Uncle Norbert?

'You're right, Mabel,' he said, looking down at the creatures playing on the ground. 'Time to do our bit.'

'What's that you say, lad?' his uncle asked, propped against the wall, still recovering from his escape.

'Something I've got to do, Uncle,' Hilton said. He looked at the sheds where so many ferrets were living in misery. 'You get your breath back, stay out of view in case Huxley is sniffing about. Come with me, you lot.'

Together, Hilton and the seven ferrets slid their way silently behind the black building until they reached the tiny escape hole with the missing vent.

'Ideas?' he asked, sizing up the gap. 'I'll never get through there. What was it like inside?'

'Row upon row of tiny, cramped cages...' Mabel started.

'Were they locked?'

'Hmmm, I didn't see padlocks like our Ferret Master uses, but they wouldn't come out, even when they saw the hole we'd made,' she said.

Couldn't or wouldn't, Hilton thought? Perhaps they were too scared to consider escaping.

'That HUGE bolt on the front door is a bit of a problem,' Jagger reminded them.

'It's much too high for me.' Hilton shrugged.

Rodders piped up. 'I've got a plan. We need Blaze's Best but let's go quietly past Our Ferret Master.'

'This is no time for eating, Rodders,' Hilton complained. But the others were off, hopping and skipping nimbly over the gravel path, following their leader back to the dingey barn.

Chapter Thirty-One – A Wheelbarrow Full of Ferrets

THE SUN SHONE SOFTLY ON the horrid place where Hilton and his uncle had been left to rot. The knot in Hilton's stomach returned as he imagined that barn door closing behind him once more, keeping him from his family and friends forever.

'Quiet,' he said, as the creatures gathered at his feet. 'What do we need to do?'

Rodders looked across the darkness. 'We're going to build you a step.'

'Build it from what?' Hilton asked, squinting around for a step ladder or an old chair.

'Sacks of Blaze's Best!' Rodders said.

'I'll never be able to carry those myself. And what if Huxley comes back?'

'Mabel, you're look-out. What's that in the corner, Ferret Boy?' he said, pointing his wet nose towards the shadowy space where a single red handle was the only thing that could be seen. 'It's a Blaze-Shifter!'

'It's a wheelbarrow, Rodders. Same thing. Let's give it a go.'

As the boy heaved his first sack of food into the red barrow, he thought Rodders' plan might work. He had watched his father lug heavy bags of compost around their garden, lifting by corners that resembled ears, and as long as they were quiet, a couple of bags should be enough.

'Bag number one!' he said, hoisting up the handles as the hobs rushed to the front wheels and pushed upward, taking some of the weight on their furry little shoulders. Hilton gripped until his knuckles were white and his arms shook with the strain. 'Stay between the wheels,' he muttered. 'We can't have any casualties today.'

Carefully, he steered the barrow, which seemed to have a will of its own, to the Black Shed. He paused, checking side to side, making sure Huxley was nowhere in sight.

'That's my job!' Mabel said. 'Don't you trust me, Ferret Boy?'

'Build your step, boy. They're waiting,' Rodders reminded him.

AFTER TWO MORE NERVE-WRACKING visits to the barn, the step made from Blaze's Best was ready for Hilton. 'While I'm trying the bolt,' he said, 'go in through the vent, and warn them. We can't have any noise. See what's keeping them in their cages.'

Mabel watched the boy wobble precariously on the stacked sacks, gritting her pointy teeth and looking away each time a fall looked likely. Hilton pulled and tugged at the bolt, but it would not move. His face tightened trying to release it and his jaw ached.

'Needs oil,' he said.

'Stay there,' Mabel told him. 'There's some in the barn with the tools.'

Before Hilton could open his mouth, she was gone.

Chapter Thirty-Two – The Lock-In

AS HILTON BALANCED ON THE sacks, he heard a noise of the most unwelcome type. Footsteps, the human kind, crunched through the gravel along the side of the shed. He jumped silently from his perch and darted to the other side of the Black Shed where he pressed his tired body against the warm metal wall. His heart pounded like a steam train, and he tuned in his bat ears for clues.

Was it his uncle or the hateful Huxley lurking around the corner? Uncle Norbert would be strong enough to pull the bolt and release the ferrets, but…it could be Huxley…

…on

…the

…prowl.

A big, fat lump stuck in Hilton's throat. He waited, trying to swallow it down.

A mobile phone sounded across the gloomy Spine Acre buildings. It played a tune the boy knew only too well. Hilton's dad sung it often. '*We're In The Money*' it trilled.

We're in the money, Let's spend it, lend it, send it, rollin' along.

The big, knotted lump was squashed down into Hilton's chest. There was nothing about that tune made him happy.

'Can't it wait?' the gruff voice said to whoever was calling. It was, without doubt, the horrible Huxley.

As the heat of the building transferred into Hilton's trousers, his bottom was getting warmer and warmer. He was either going to have to move, or to shout as he imagined the back of his pants start to sizzle. He shuffled quietly away from the wall where he stood, terrified, and part grilled.

'Well, if it's urgent, but it's not a good time,' he could hear Huxley saying, as his footsteps crunched across the gravel, getting ever so slightly quieter with each pace.

Hilton breathed out a big sigh, releasing his knot out onto the warm breeze. Mabel was back at his feet, the nozzle of a small oilcan clenched between her fierce teeth. He jumped onto his step of food sacks and dripped the oil onto the sticky bolt.

After a little twisting and turning, it slid back, and the door swung open. Row upon row of black metal cages were revealed, each containing a beautifully conditioned but very miserable animal.

'They said you were about to set us free,' the one in the first cage said. It looked Hilton up and down. 'You don't look…well, tall enough to be a Ferret Master.'

'*He's* Number One Junior Handler,' Mabel bragged, 'and he looks after us very well.' Hilton blushed. He wasn't used to people or ferrets, saying nice things about him.

It felt good.

'What's your name? he asked. 'We've not much time.'

'We're numbers,' the ferret replied. 'I'm 101. We have names for the festivals, but back in the Black Shed, we are numbers once more.'

'Then tell me, 101, how to unlock your cages.'

'Can't be done,' the ferret said, sadly. 'He tells us the best electronic system is keeping us 'safe'. No metal locks or bolts. The Master has a swipe card for that machine. The doors unlock together. No-one has ever escaped from Spine Acre Farm.'

Chapter Thirty-Three – An Electronic Wizz

'WE'VE COME TOO FAR TO give up,' Mabel said. 'There has to be a way.'

'I don't know anything about electronics,' Hilton sighed. 'And even if Uncle did, he wouldn't approve of setting you free. It's a dangerous world out there for unaccompanied ferrets.'

'We'd take our chances,' said 101. 'We wish we had a Master like yours.'

Rodders whispered something in Hilton's ear. 'Unless,' Hilton continued, 'you would agree to make your way to his place, East Northumbria Ferret Boarding and Welfare Society? We can make space for you all there.'

'Have you checked that out with the Master?' Jagger asked. Hilton was not about to.

'Anything! Just get us out,' 101 pleaded, as Hilton stared at the electronic box. How to get Huxley's swipe card and release the creatures?

'I was accidentally concentrating at school once when Miss Sharkey explained circuits…and what did she say…where there's a circuit, there's a power supply, and…where there's a power supply, there are… WIRES! So, Ferret Friends,' he went on, 'where are the wires that power this box?'

Very soon, Norbert's lads and lasses were enjoying that special treat, the one Norbert would never allow: gnawing through deliciously meaty, wonderfully stringy cables full of plastic and rubber and metal wire. The chewier the better. Their sharp little teeth soon gnashed through the spaghetti of flexes feeding the box.

Then, suddenly, there was…

… a bright blue flash.

Silence fell over the cages. Everyone looked at Jagger.

His fur stood on edge, his floof poofed to make him look twice his usual size and quite scary. Like a Ferret Frankenstein to be exact. He stood, locked in his spiky position as still as a stuffed hedgehog. Hundreds of pairs of beady black eyes cast around the shed.

They held their warm ferret breath.

'Had more volts than that and lived to tell the tale,' Jagger sniggered, shaking out his spiny pelt and waggling his way back to Hilton. 'Hear that? It's the sound of free will!'

The cage doors popped open to reveal a fright of ferrets.

Timidly, the creatures made their way to the cage doors, sniffing the air in front of them. It tasted of countryside, happiness and freedom.

'Just one minute,' Hilton whispered, holding up his hand. 'Someone's coming.'

That fateful tune, *I'm In The Money,* was lilting happily across the farm buildings.

'He's on his way back!' Hilton said.

'Knew it was too good to be true,' 101 said, shaking his head.

'I'll close the door, put everything back. He won't even know I've been,' Hilton replied.

'We're still trapped,' 101 said, sadly.

'Your cages are open. See that little vent at the back? That's your escape route. See you at East Northumbria.'

Hilton edged back the black metal door, shutting in their new friends for the last time. They wheeled the Blaze's Best to the rear of the shed, a tasty snack for the escapees as they prepared to flee their horrid captor. The wheelbarrow was abandoned as the gang slinked back to Uncle Norbert.

He was tapping the cracked glass of his watch, asking what time they thought it was. 'Time to get out of here, Uncle,' Hilton smiled, as his furry friends darted ahead.

Chapter Thirty-Four – A Car on the Road

AS DARKNESS FELL AROUND THEM, Uncle Norbert said it was safe to move into the open.

Leaving the high wall where they'd hidden, they quickly found the road that had taken them to Huxley's miserable empire and decided to follow the bus route back towards the Ferret Boarding and Welfare Society. Silence surrounded them. The only noises, their own footsteps echoing in the dark, and the hooting of an owl in the distance.

'They've gone mighty quiet, Uncle. Think they're alright?' Hilton said, squinting into the distance as the Ferret Five leapt along in front of them, their stretched bodies creating waves of fur on the shiny surface of the road.

'They're minding their own business, lad,' his uncle replied.

'It *is* a business, Uncle. The name for a collection of ferrets.'

'What's that you say, boy?'

'A collective noun, you know?'

'How can you collect nouns in the dark?' the old man tutted. 'I'll leave *that sort of business* to you and your teachers.'

Hilton was not quite sure how to break the news – of Huxley's released animals all scrambling their way to his uncle's premises at this very moment in time. *That* was going to be quite a deal.

THE LONG ROAD STRETCHED AHEAD. Hilton's legs were tired and his eyes sore. He was desperate to get back to his uncle's rows of wonderfully wonky, topsy-turvy, higgledy-piggledy sheds and the clever creatures that lived there.

He was quite keen to speak to his mum and dad too. Although he should probably let Uncle Norbert explain about their trip to Spine Acre Farm.

In the darkness, it was difficult to know exactly where they were, but Hilton used the bus stops and counted back to help work out how much further to go. His uncle looked worn out and was still carrying Ogden and Rubina, who were silent.

'This is where the Potato Woman got on, Uncle Norbert,' he said, as they approached the third bus shelter.

'A woman made from potatoes?' Uncle Norbert looked blank. 'Your Aunt Izolda, now, she made the most beautiful, buttery mashed potato,' he said, sounding wistful as his tummy rumbled like thunder in the night's silence.

They were halfway home.

Hilton started to think about a cup of tea... some lovely, hot fish and chips with salt and vinegar ...and hearing his mum's voice.

He would do better from now, he promised himself. And he would tell her the same.

Their energy was almost totally gone and their feet starting to drag when they heard the sound of a car engine. 'Dunno which direction it's coming from,' Hilton said, checking along the road.

His uncle shook his head. His face was pale. 'What if Huxley's checked the barn?' Hilton said, watching the old man's expression. 'He might already know we've ...'

There was another awful thought swirling around inside Hilton's head. His uncle was unaware that, at this very moment, the Black Shed ferrets were running free somewhere.

Somewhere quite near. And making their way to the East Northumbria Ferret Boarding and Welfare Society. This was something he must confess when the time was right. But not now.

'Just what I was thinking, lad, unless Mabel managed to nip the ignition wires on his car. Let's squeeze into the bus shelter until it passes.'

Through the trees and hedgerows, headlights approached from behind, and they huddled together in the suffocating darkness of the brick bus stop. 'Breathe like you were in the barn again, lad.'

The ferrets disappeared behind the wall as Norbert hid the carrier from sight. Headlights swept around the corner, their huge beams searching the darkness, illuminating each blade of grass, every bump in the road. The pair dared not look out from their hiding place.

The car engine slowed. And then…

…stopped.

Their hearts quickened. Hilton stared at his uncle. Should they take flight, run for their lives? The old man shook his head. Hilton understood. He was still.

The car drew level, its colour concealed by the darkness. The driver's door swung open, and a man stepped out. He walked towards the huddle.

'Norbert, lad?' came a voice. 'What's happened to you? We were worried.'

'Long story, Morris,' Norbert puffed.

'Jump in, the lot of you!' Mr Morrison said, and together with the carrier and the ferrets appearing from behind the brickwork, they squeezed onto the back seat of the car.

They began to tell the Morrisons their incredible story as they chugged off towards home.

'We tried to ring,' Mrs Morrison said. 'Wanted to book Jonty and Jasper in for boarding next week, but the line was dead. When we called round, the place was abandoned. We knew you wouldn't leave your place like that, Norbert. But *that's* incredible.'

Almost as incredible as my heroic actions in The Black Shed, Hilton thought. But this was still not the right time.

As Mr Morrison's car tootled up the narrow lane, his headlights lit up the old place, and the uncle and nephew smiled in relief.

'You need a good night's sleep. Ring the police in the morning,' Mr Morrison told them. 'Oh, your phone's not working, is it? I'll come over early. Use my mobile.' He opened the car doors and let out Mrs Morrison, who insisted on giving them a huge, breath-extinguishing hug while her husband lifted out the ferret carrier containing Ogden and Rubina.

'Glad you're all home safely,' she said.

Hilton looked around. He seemed a little distracted. 'Hang on …hang on a minute,' he replied. 'We're not all here. One of our ferrets is missing, there's only four loose.'

He dropped his head to look beneath the car seats, then under the car. 'Who's gone? Oh no! It's Rodders.'

Chapter Thirty-Five – Eagles and Badgers and Hawks, Oh My!

'THERE'S NO POINT DRIVING AROUND in the dark to look for him,' Mrs Morrison said. 'He could be anywhere.'

She was right. It wasn't a long journey for a human but for a ferret, it was halfway around the world and back. It was impossible to see him, and he'd only been along that road tucked inside a carrier. He'd have no idea of the best way home, Hilton thought.

If he made it.

A Walk in the Wild- A Field Guide had informed Hilton ferrets were a great source of food for hawks and badgers. Rodders' journey might have come to a sudden and very sad end.

'We'll look in the morning,' Uncle Norbert suggested, pulling a face that meant there was little hope. 'Until then, we better make sure this lot is safe.' They'd have to make the sheds more secure, he told Hilton, but not until tomorrow when they could visit Bingley's to buy extra locks.

And Hilton was imagining doing that tomorrow only to find new ferret families taking up residence in his uncle's already crowded accommodation. How would he explain that?

For tonight, one night only, the Ferret Six would stay in the house, three in each bedroom to share out the smell that might follow in the morning.

HILTON SLEPT LIKE A LOG.

As he went downstairs next day, his uncle was at the breakfast table looking sad at the Oaty Flakes box, waiting for Rodders to appear and tip it over. 'There's *one* good piece of news,' the old man said. 'I tried the phone, and Huxley must've unplugged it. I've called the Morrisons. You can speak to your mum when you're ready.'

'Let's leave it a while,' Hilton said. 'Can we look for Rodders as soon as the sheds are done?'

TOGETHER, THE UNCLE AND HIS nephew decided that the trip to Bingley's would include a tour of Dalworthy and the country roads where Rodders went missing. And that ringing Hilton's mum and dad was best left 'til tea-time when they would be home together.

In between, perhaps the right opportunity would allow Hilton to tell his uncle about the ferrets he had released from Huxley's horrible clutches. He was sure Uncle Norbert would understand completely.

But, there were *quite* a lot of ferrets. A considerable number, in fact.

THERE WERE PLENTY OF LOCKS for sale at Bingley's, and even more Christmas trees than last time, as they walked through the festive aisle together, transferring glitter from the floor to their shoes, planning the best way to cover the search area for Rodders.

There was no Blaze's Best as they passed through the pet department, but they knew that, and Hilton decided that Bingley's was not the place to tackle a tricky conversation. And, not all the ferrets *would* find their own way to East Northumbria Ferret Boarding and Welfare Society, he hoped.

THE TOUR OF DALWORTHY LASTED as long as it took Uncle Norbert's car to almost run out of petrol, and the conversation turned to the number of miles left before the old girl would splutter to a halt, and they'd have to walk home again.

Although they scanned the hedgerows and the ditches, looked out over the fields and the streams and called his name quietly, so they didn't attract attention to themselves, or bump into Huxley, the pair decided reluctantly, that according to *A Walk in the Wild- A Field Guide*, Rodders could be making a new, free life for himself, hopefully with a black-footed jill. Or, Hilton thought, maybe with a ferret released from Spine Acre Farm.

But, definitely not with an eagle or a hawk.

White-tailed eagle, Haliaeetus albicilla, page 42. Has a fully feathered, often crested head and strong feet equipped with great curved talons (poor Rodders). *Eagles subsist mainly on live prey. Too weighty for effective aerial pursuit, they try to surprise and overwhelm their prey on the ground* (poor, poor Rodders).

AS THE BRANCHES UP THE narrow lane scraped the green paint of Norbert's car, Hilton held tightly onto the packet of forget-me-knot seeds bought to remember their missing pal. The blue flowers would remind them of their best boy and bring them happy memories. They thought about his bravery, alone in the countryside.

'I've got just the thing to plant them in,' Uncle Norbert said, as they got out the car. He tramped off through the sheds, leaving Hilton alone at the door to Bluebell Lodge.

'Psst.' It was a hissing noise. Hilton looked at his uncle's car.

Then, it happened again. 'Pssst…psst….'

As Hilton walked around the vehicle, checking it out for the old man, a cheeky panda face appeared from between the wheels.

Then another, a white furry face. And one more. A black mask with white whiskers.

'This is the right place, Ferret Boy?' a squeaky voice asked. It was 101, and he had possibly 102 and 103 by his side. Little quizzical eyes appeared from nowhere and were suddenly all staring at Hilton.

'This is it. This is it!' he could hear them squeal. 'We found it!'

He gulped. Oh crikey, he thought.

'Look,' he said. 'I'm pleased you're safe, but I've got to make proper arrangements for you. So can you just....'

The sound of his uncle's heavy footsteps lumbering towards them made him lower his voice to barely a whisper. '....hang out somewhere until I sort it out?'

'Got them!' the old man shouted. As Hilton turned round, Norbert produced, from his shovel-sized hands, a pair of old wellington boots, and the scissors from inside the porch. The boy had no idea what his uncle was planning as he hurled the boots through the air towards him.

But as the missiles landed, there was not a ferret in sight.

In a sunny spot in front of the house, Uncle Norbert knelt on the ground. He cut a big chunk from the length of each wellington boot. Then, he carefully peeled back the rest, to create an ankle length version.

Hilton was still puzzled.

The old man used the scissors to puncture three holes in the sole of each boot, and he nodded as his nephew looked on. He collected handfuls of soil and dropped them into the wellingtons until they were full to their brims.

'Plant pots,' he said. 'One from me, one from you. Sprinkle on your seeds. I'll get the watering can.'

It was heavy, made of a dull silver metal gone rusty, and the end of the spout had dropped off leaving a rotten edge over which the water splashed and sprayed, soaking their boots, the seeds and everything else around. 'It's something to remember Rodders by,' the old man said.

The pair stood silently, admiring their work when out of the corner of his eye, Hilton saw a flash of movement. Bushy busy movement, to be exact. And he realised he was about to be found out. Before he could tell Uncle Norbert about The Black Shed at Spine Acre Farm.

The streak of fur caught their gaze. And as they stared, a ferret, very dirty, quite thin, stood looking up at the man and boy. It had one red eye, and one brown.

'Rodders!' they said together. 'Where have *you* been?'

Chapter Thirty-Six – Time to Come Clean

RAV'S FISH AND CHIPS WERE bought for tea, and the pair enjoyed every single chip, every morsel of crispy batter and mouthful of succulent white fish splashed with salt and vinegar. Rodders had all the crinkly ends not big enough to call a chip.

Uncle Norbert and Hilton discussed they could no longer delay the dreaded phone call to his parents. 'Let me do the talking, lad. When everything's sorted, I'll pass you over to your mum.'

And Hilton worried that he could no longer put off telling his uncle a large number of nameless ferrets released from Spine Acre Farm were currently navigating their whiskery way through the northern countryside, desperate for new homes at East Northumbria Ferret Boarding and Welfare Society.

'DONNA? YES, YES, a problem with the phone, that's all. The stoats? They're *ferrets*, Donna. Ah...... winding me up...... Yeah.... Very funny. Bit of an update for you....We were across at Spine Acre Farm yesterday, the lad and me.....Huxley put an offer on the table....no, not the real table....He wanted to become partners....oh Donna, you know what I mean... He thought that after our wins at Bagley, I might want to join forces with him. He asked me to give it serious thought.....and then let him know....So we went over, rather than talk on the phone...It seemed a more sensible idea.....but, since Hilton's been helping, I think we're better by ourselves…He's got a real talent, your lad….and there's some great news for you in that department, so I was hoping he could stay longer, you know, to help me get the lads and lasses ready for the National Championships at the end of September…I think things are set to take off again, and I could be back at the top of the tree…Like a pine marten, Donna? No, not like that at all…I'll put Hilton on…here, lad…'

The roll of the old man's eyes was all Hilton needed as the phone handset with its big cream curly wire was passed his way. A pine marten. He'd not cast eyes on a pine marten, *Martes martes, page 15,* out here in Northumbria. Something else to look forward to.

HILTON REPLACED THE HANDSET ON the telephone. His head was down.

'Was your mum pleased about the Best Junior Handler award?' Norbert asked, smiling widely. It had been a good day after all. They were home safely, the ferrets were more secure than ever, and Rodders was alive and well.

'I've got to go home in two days,' the boy said. 'School starts again the day after.'

Chapter Thirty-Seven – The Welfare Society

'I'VE POURED YOUR OATY FLAKES, Uncle,' Hilton said next morning, as he sidled up to that familiar green woolly cardigan. He took in a deep, deep breath. 'I've done something very silly. I can't go back to school and leave things like this.'

'*Things?*' the old man said, putting down his spoon with a noisy clink on the flowery blue bowl. 'What sort of *things?*'

This was not going to be easy, Hilton realised, but before he could open his mouth...

'One second, son. There's the phone again, probably another booking for the boarding. It's really taking off again.'

Not easy at all.

'Ah, how many creatures did you say?' Hilton could hear his uncle question the person on the other end of the phone. 'And they're from Spine Acre Farm?'

Hilton gulped. He was about to be found out. Before he could come clean.

The old man replaced the handset with a heavy clunk. 'Well, there's a turn up for the books,' he said. 'Apparently, someone's broken into one of Huxley's sheds and released his ferrets into the wild.' He eyed the boy up and down.

Very slowly, the uncle's gaze moved across his nephew's face, checking in on his right eye, then his left. Hilton could feel his cheeks flushing. His mouth was suddenly as dry as the box of Oaty Flakes.

'That was the Police. They think it was probably an animal activist, you know, one of those animal rights people. They think the ferrets might find their way here. Bit of a long shot. Don't you think?'

And the old man watched Hilton, measuring his reaction carefully, very carefully, the boy thought, as he gave out that particular piece of news. Hilton wriggled on his chair.

A train of heat travelled up from his toes, calling in at his knees, his tummy, making him clear his throat and pulling in to rest very firmly on his now rosy, red cheeks. Here was a great opportunity. The subject of released ferrets at the breakfast table.

Ready for him to share his guilty secret. Or, a chance to dodge the blame, let the 'anonymous activist' take responsibility…What to do? Hilton pondered.

'The strange thing is…' Uncle Norbert continued before Hilton could speak, 'I've been catching glimpses of new faces all around the place. Wondered where they were coming from.'

And they both knew. Hilton's chest suddenly felt much better and he could breathe easily once more. 'Thing is, as ownership can't be proved, they've asked if I've the space to take in any wanderers. A kind of rescue mission. How about that, Hilton?'

Chapter Thirty-Eight – No Time for Numbers

'I'VE BEEN THINKING. IT'S time, lad,' Uncle Norbert said a few days later as they finished up their cleaning routine once more. With an increased number of animals, the chores felt endless and the pair were getting tired. 'Maybe it's the right opportunity to be rid of the numbers.'

Hilton felt a moment of panic.

Although there was more to do, they were managing. There was the odd squabble among the Spine Acre escapees, like the time number 76 and number 34 tussled over the spare grapes. But, as they adapted to being together in his uncle's sheds instead of their high-tech metal cages, when the National Championships came, there were many more critters to choose from, to train and to groom for their starring roles. There was more talent for each event and that had to be a good thing.

Hadn't his uncle agreed to take in the Spine Acre ferrets for good? To look after them, as his own? Perhaps Hilton had misunderstood, but the thought of parting with the animals, now they were settling and looking like they belonged, made his knees wobble and his tummy drop.

What would happen to them now? *He'd* never release them, and he didn't believe his uncle would either. No adventures involving

...ret Fraudster, eagles or badgers for them. The only ...itement Hilton wanted was the National Championships.

The alternatives were all worse. Much worse.

'We can't go on like this, lad,' the old man said, plonking himself down on the step at the shed door and pushing his smeary glasses back up onto his stubbly-haired nose. 'Any suggestions?'

The boy's mind was overrun by ideas, none of them good. Sell some? Rehome a few at the National Championships? Try the vets in Dalworthy? Was there anyone who'd like to train their very own furry inchworm?

None of Hilton's suggestions seemed fair to the animals, so he kept his mouth closed and shrugged his shoulders as the old man looked at him.

'I was thinking of the Bible,' Uncle Norbert said.

'Sorry, Uncle?'

Hilton was totally confused. How could a Bible help get rid of extra ferrets? He began to wonder whether his uncle was quite well.

'We've pinched names from rock stars and politicians, but nothing from the Bible yet.'

'Names?'

'Well, we can't go on calling these lads and lasses by numbers! It's just not right.'

AFTER TEA, HILTON WAS SENT upstairs to look under the bed where he was told he'd find Aunt Izolda's Bible.

By the end of that day, the numbers had gone, and in a naming ceremony that was very informal, just the man, the boy and a large number of furry creatures, number 76 became Joshua, number 55 turned into Zachary, and number 43 looked like a Grace. The old man had carried a pail of water from shed to shed which swung and slopped as they worked their way around. He insisted on splodging a wet dot on the forehead of each Spine Acre animal, 'baptising' it the same way he'd done for every other of his East Northumbria lads and lasses. The only hiccup occurred when Hilton had suggested 'Isobel' for jill number 25 and realised when his uncle took in a deep breath, that it was too close to that name, Izolda, and so he'd quickly changed it.

'She looks more like a Ruth, I think.'

Chapter Thirty-Nine – Back to School

IT WAS A PROMISE HILTON was happy to make his mum and dad. It was the only way things might work for everyone, Norbert suggested.

The thought of returning home was fine. The boy was keen to see his parents after the events of the summer at the East Northumbria Ferret Boarding and Welfare Society. But what Hilton couldn't face was the idea of seeing less of Uncle Norbert and of the cute creatures he had come to love and trust. They had saved his life at Spine Acre Farm, and things continued to go very well with the ferrets for some reason.

Perhaps because of the Blaze's Best they were being fed. Hilton couldn't be sure.

Uncle Norbert was quick to make the suggestion when Hilton's mum was on the phone that day, so it seemed he wanted the boy to continue his work and keep up the success they were having.

'I know he can't *stay*, Donna, and *he knows he's got to go back to school...*' Hilton had rolled his eyes. 'But, he's so good with the lads and lasses. With the National Championships coming up, he could do really well....Isn't that what we all wanted? Things are ready to take off for us here. We've increased our numbers; we're building more sheds. What if the lad came to help every weekend?'

Hilton had nodded enthusiastically. He had held up both thumbs. Only weekends? Better than nothing, he supposed.

'And I know he'll stick in at school and do as good a job there as he's doing here…' He looked across at the boy and held him in that serious, checking sort of gaze. It was Hilton's turn to roll his eyes.

'….but it's what everyone wants, and the National Championships are *only* once a year. It's a great chance, for Hilton, for me *and* for the business. Have I ever told you that's the name for a group of ferrets, Donna? A business, get it? Well, no matter… but, *that* would work, wouldn't it?'

Hilton was nodding, mouthing to his uncle, '….and I'll come after school too. I'll get the bus.' It was a great result. The best to be achieved.

HILTON WENT TO EAST NORTHUMBRIA Ferret Boarding and Welfare Society every day after school, and his mum or dad would take him on Friday night and collect him each Sunday evening. Their chats in the car were always about ferrets, not stoats, not pine martens, not skunks, and most definitely not weasels.

Each week, Hilton's mum and dad saw the improvements Norbert was making to his place, buying a whole new shed here, repairing the broken ones properly with good quality materials there, and even talking about redecorating his bedroom.

With his wins at the Bagley Ferret Festival, his boarding customers were returning *and* buying more animals from him, he said. *Business* was getting better.

HILTON DIDN'T WANT ANYTHING TO get in the way of helping Uncle Norbert. He stuck to his side of the bargain at school. One afternoon, Miss Sharkey asked his mum to come in at the end of the day. She was well-named, Miss Sharkey.

Cetorhinus maximus, basking shark, page 66. Its fierce looks belie the fact it feeds only on plankton. Swimming slowly, with its large mouth wide open, it is a social creature, gathering in groups or 'schools'.

Hilton's eyes darted around the classroom. Was the plan about to come crashing down around his head? What had he done wrong?

He racked his brain. No apples. No shoes. No squirrel. He honestly couldn't think of...

one...

single...

thing.

'Sit down, Mrs Hughes,' Miss Sharkey said, pointing to a chair she'd placed next to her.

'Do you want me to wait outside, Miss?' Hilton asked. His throat was very dry and scratchy.

'No Hilton. You need to hear this,' she said, taking her seat and smiling as the mother and son sat together. 'I don't want to wait until parents' evening to tell you about Hilton, Mrs Hughes. I dealt with him a lot last year, on the yard mainly, and I don't know what I was expecting, but it wasn't this.'

She went on to tell Hilton's mum he'd changed over the summer and was being well behaved and working as hard as he could, which was harder than she was expecting. In fact, he was a pleasure to teach, she said, as she showed them the door and asked Hilton to keep on doing whatever made the difference.

'He's told us so many ferret stories since he came back to school, and the one about the loose ferret that climbed up the lady's skirt.....well...well, I don't know what's happened over the summer, but I'm liking the new improved Hilton,' she said.

His mum was silent until they were in the car, when she turned and smiled at him, saying, 'Yeah, we like that Hilton too.'

As she turned the car back into their street, she said, 'A ferret up some woman's skirt, Hilton? Are you kidding?'

Chapter Forty – Good Calls, Bad Calls

HILTON CONTINUED WITH HIS PLAN. He had used the harnesses and leads at first. Started with the ferrets he knew best.

He had cleared a grassy patch he called his training ring at the back of the sheds, not knowing whether his Uncle Norbert would agree with what he was doing, but it was not a lot different to the activities in the festivals; the mazes, the races, and the ferrets enjoyed working together. He had remembered Mabel and Rubina's prize winning performances and created his plan to help the animals work together by watching lots of dog training programmes.

'STAY!' his mum had heard him shout from his bedroom while he was meant to be doing his homework one day.

'Who? Stay where?' she replied, and he realised the words he thought were glued inside his brain were actually fluttering out of his mouth. He bit his tongue. He had almost given the game away.

'I hope you're not thinking about asking for a dog, Hilton,' she'd said. 'We've enough with you and the ferrets.'

IT WAS DIFFICULT AT FIRST. Like concentrating at school. But he really did want to succeed in these lessons. His Ferret Mastery Classes.

It started in a small way. Teaching Ogden and Jagger to SIT and STAY, and having others from Bluebell Lodge watch, see how it should be done by the older, wiser ferrets.

Then, rewards. Lots of Blaze's Best. And Oaty Flakes. Grapes.

Hilton realised the critters were quick to learn. They watched patiently until they were released from their carrier or box and encouraged to join in, and the nuggets of food made it all worthwhile.

When the SIT and STAY became easy, Hilton moved to the next stage of his plan. He was a little more nervous about this. He trusted them to SIT and STAY, but as he backed away, keeping their cheeky little faces in view, there were anxious moments when he wondered whether they would all come when called.

What if they didn't? Suppose they ran off in different directions? Then, who would he chase first, and would he dare tell Uncle Norbert?

But the Ferret Boy had no need to worry. He quickly learned the animals were happy to do his bidding, reward or not. They all came when that scary single syllable left his lips. 'COME.'

'I think you're wasting your time, lad,' his uncle would say as he passed the training ground with another bucket of feed, 'but, if it makes you happy and keeps you busy…' And happy indeed was what it made Hilton.

He created a longer list of tricks for them to learn, and as they completed each one, he became bolder in finding ways to organise them, coming out of the sheds when he whistled, lining up, making a circle, holding onto one another's tails as they ran.

And then he decided upon his masterpiece. It would be difficult, but he was sure they could do it. It took days to master.

Larger, stronger ones on the bottom row and building through size and weight, until the lightest and smallest creatures were perched on top. Hilton and his fuzzbutts had created a perfect pyramid of funny ferretness, like he'd seen done on TV with jugglers or motorbikes, but never with animals.

'WHERE DID YOU LEARN TO do that, lad?' Uncle Norbert said, standing back and scratching his head. In the field at the back of the sheds, Hilton had a gathering. A circle of creatures, too many to count, all with their own names. They surrounded him.

None of them moved.

In every colour of fur, with every shade of eyes, and with differing lengths of whiskers, they watched. Silent and still.

'I saw it on a dog show,' Hilton said, keeping his eyes firmly on the assembly, all looking his way. 'Can't quite get them to BEG. I think their body shape is all wrong, cos they wobble over, but they're good at SIT and STAY. Aren't they, Uncle?'

'You'll need those skills, the number we've got now,' the old man said, casting his eyes across their new sheds, constructed from this and that. 'No problem getting them all together?'

'None at all. When I open the shed doors and whistle, they just come. They never run off.'

'Well, you've managed something I could never do,' his uncle said, an empty Blaze's sack flapping in his hand as he started to walk back towards the house.

He paused momentarily and turned to the boy. 'I had another of those funny phone calls this morning.'

His uncle had mentioned the same thing happening a few days ago, and they had discussed the possibility of Huxley trying to find out where his animals were and claim them back.

'The ones where no-one speaks?' Hilton asked. 'Probably someone playing a joke, Uncle. Or a wrong number.'

Chapter Forty-One – The Yellow Car Returns

'WE NEED TO BE ALERT,' Hilton said to the gathering when his uncle was out of earshot. 'Anyone got news?'

The ferret that was previously 101, now named Asher, piped up. 'The Ferret Fiend's on the warpath. A passing stoat heard he wants his animals back for the Championships. He knows exactly where we are, he says.'

A chorus of hisses and chatters ran through the masses. Some of them started to shiver and quake. 'We're not going back. We're never going back!' they chanted.

'We've practised our defences, the stuff Uncle hasn't seen,' Hilton reminded them. 'Just remember your moves when the time comes.'

He cast his eyes across the field as a sleek yellow car travelled up the road, slowing at the end of the lane.

'And this might be the very moment we were expecting,' he said quietly. 'So, as we rehearsed, get into your camouflage positions.' Within a nano-second, every single ferret had gone from his sight.

HILTON MADE HIS WAY ACROSS the field, staying in the hedgerow and behind the messy bushes framing the drive. His heart dropped as he watched the car door swing open and the bony knee of a long, skinny leg swung out. A big brown moccasin shoe hit the ground.

Then, the tall dark-haired man unfolded himself like Uncle Norbert's clothes horse, and emerged from the low driver's seat, pulling himself up to his full height and straightening down his dark clothes.

A large gristly knot tied itself in the boy's stomach as he realised this was, in fact, *that* very moment. Huxley was back.

Chapter Forty-Two – A Force of Ferrets

HILTON'S EYES SWIVELLED.

Ahead, Huxley was walking up the drive, diving behind the bushes and trees that attacked the cars daring to pass. He checked over his shoulder every now and then, making sure no-one was watching.

No-one except Hilton. What would Huxley do this time?

The horrid human skulked past the house and flattened his skinny frame into every doorway, the shade absorbing his long, black coat, and highlighting his pale, narrow face and prominent nose. Staying just a few paces behind the Ferret Fraudster, Hilton did the same, tracking the evil man's path through his uncle's business.

One by one, Huxley approached each shed, easing open the door, looking around and peering inside. When he didn't find what he was looking for, he closed it silently and prowled his way to the next.

After invading four sheds containing no ferrets at all, Hilton heard a low grumble. As the raider moved on through the premises, 'Where *has* he put them?' came his thunderous question. Between Crocus Cottage and Apple Blossom Bungalow the man paused to look across at that same field where Hilton had spent so much time with the East Northumbria Combined Ferret Force.

It had been a struggle at first, getting names for all the poor critters that had answered only to numbers, trusting them to play and train together without nipping or squabbling or stealing one another's food. But, over time, Hilton had seen it happen, his ferret army working as one, listening for his instructions and following every word.

'You saved us, Ferret Boy,' they said, happy to be alive, happier to be loved.

The field had been a place of Hilton's despair and delight. Of watching his work and training pay off as his band of raggle-taggle, scraggety-baggety faintly scruffy and previously whiffy creatures absorbed their new friends and became one.

The East Northumbria Ferret Force.

Hilton's cheerful memories deflated as his nemesis stepped out from behind Apple Blossom Bungalow, and the stealthy trail continued. For his plan to work, he needed to get Huxley onto the field.

Taking care not to be seen, Hilton pulled bite-sized pieces of Blaze's Best and skimmed them, one by one, across the grass, at different angles and varying speeds, ruffling the lush blades a little until it caught the invader's eye. With a snap of his head, he homed in on the movement and fixed his beady gaze on the ground.

Hilton's ferret friends didn't let him down.

No sooner did the pellets land, than one creature at a time would raise its head, just eyes and ears above the grass, to nip the food away, visible for only a ferrety fraction of a second.

First, it was Joseph. Then Hannah. Eli took the next. The little heads popped and nodded, bobbed and dipped, drawing Huxley closer to the spot where the mighty moves had been practised.

Every creature knew what to do. If only Hilton could manipulate the monster into position.

'CATCH,' he whispered. Come on, Asher. This is your time, he thought. Remember when you were 101? He skimmed another pellet across the grass in Asher's direction.

Spotting the mini panda face he knew only too well, the man stopped and pulled himself to his scariest height. He muttered furiously beneath his breath, 'One hundred and one! I knew it was you! I've *got* you now!'

Hilton remembered the set pieces they had rehearsed, and he took in a long deep breath as he issued the first command.

'DOWN!' he shouted.

Suddenly, waves of fur appeared from nowhere and lapped around the feet of the intruder as he walked, the squirmy bodies blocking his way and causing him to stumble.

'Argh! What are you doing?' Huxley yelled, as Asher's partner in crime, previously 102 and now named Beulah, bit the bony back of his awful ankles. He wobbled and wavered on the grassy slope, but it was no good. Tumbling to the ground like a bag of loosely connected bones, he clattered and rolled on the slope.

'ROLL OVER!'

The ferrets had remembered what to do.

One by one, they leapt upon the now-scruffy black coat, jumping and nudging as they landed, spinning the villain further and further away from the sheds they now called home. As the slope steepened, his lanky body gathered speed, his arms and legs whipping out at odd angles like windmill sails as he travelled against his will, pushed and shoved by the force of ferrets. Harder and harder they used their noses, their paws and sometimes their teeth to keep Huxley on a roll, moving down the hill.

The creatures had to dodge and weave as they enjoyed this new game, their previous owner revolving like an unravelling Swiss roll towards the bottom of the hill.

A ferret version of a human festival. Without any fun for the humans. Or the prizes.

'WAIT!'

As the fraudster's lanky body gathered speed down the incline, it was time to let everyone take part. They might never get another chance for revenge.

'OKAY!'

Each ferret raised its head from their hiding position and scuttled with joy to be part of it. Huxley had no defence. Dizzy and disorientated, he came to a sudden stop in the hedge at the bottom of the hill next to his parked car, the wind knocked from his chest.

Hilton ran ahead and got himself into position.

'TAKE!'

Now, in their droves, the furry fiends worked together. Their tiny paws and bendy bodies bundled the baddie to where they wanted him. He flicked and flailed his limbs in fury, but they continued, his body carried on a sea of fur waves, edging closer and closer to his bright yellow car. Jagger scuttled forward to Hilton bearing a flash of metal in his sharp white teeth. He dropped the shiny item at the boy's feet. The key to Huxley's car, thrown free from his pocket during his rotations down the field.

Once opened, they pushed the man's lanky legs into the open door, Hilton holding it ajar, as they teamed up to wedge him back into that low-slung seat. Like a nodding dog, Huxley's head thrashed forward and back as he tried to shake them off.

'Leave me alo....' he garbled. 'You'll regret this!'

'FIND IT!'

Jagger, Neville and Mabel squiggled their way through their friends into the depths of the car. In the middle, they found the gear stick and braced themselves, Jagger to the left of the handbrake, Neville to the right.

'RELEASE!'

The hobs together hoist up the flexible Mabel until she could reach the handbrake which she pushed up with a very gentle squeak of its spring.

Slowly, the car began to move. Hilton watched its progress. He needed to judge the exact moment to give his next command.

'LEAVE!'

The creatures began to leap from the rolling vehicle as it started..

...quite slowly at first...

...to get up...

speed.

One by one, the furry forms bounded from the sports car as it moved a little faster down the lane. Together, they stood at the edge of the road and watched as the dazzling pineapple streak moved faster and faster, travelling in a dead straight line, and coming...

to a thudding metal-crunching stop...

against the only street light...

at the bottom of the slope.

A high-pitched car alarm sounded down the road, telling tales on its careless owner. The noise howled through the village as the ferret army assembled once more around Hilton's feet as he watched the whole picture unfold.

'COME!'

THE BOY CHEERED AS PC Grimshaw appeared from nowhere, pedalling his bicycle like fury towards the tangle of yellow metal, green lamppost and hissing hot steam escaping from the radiator. The officer pulled open the driver's door to survey the scene and Huxley's furious face was revealed.

'Had a little too much to drink, have we, Sir?' PC Grimshaw asked.

Chapter Forty-Three – The National Championships

THE WINDOWS OF THE NATIONAL Ferret Centre sparkled in the late September sunshine.

Every space in the car park was full. There were vehicles on grass verges and pavements. Cars of every colour and shape were shining in rows and lanes, except Uncle Norbert's old green banger, with its scratched sides and its ferrety air freshener.

Everyone wanted to be there, today of all days. Posters in the car park displayed what was on offer: 'NATIONAL CHAMPIONSHIPS TODAY- 22 DIFFERENT EVENTS TO WIN'

Big red wooden arrows with hand-painted signs saying, THIS WAY TO THE SHOWRINGS, were displayed around the outside. Owners carried their ferrets in containers made of plastic or wicker, in mesh crates and cardboard boxes. No one seemed to mind.

The uncle and nephew had bathed their lads and lasses the day before, and dried them carefully, letting them play in their hammocks while waiting their turn. Uncle Norbert was looking his smartest too; clean and tidy, the green woolly cardigan mended, and wearing his best un-bald cord trousers.

Hilton's tummy fluttered as he watched the doors to the showring. His mum and dad had promised to come.

The head judge stepped up to the microphone.

'Ferret folks of Great Britain,' he started, 'we've the makings of a great day ahead. Lots of talent in the room …and… almost as much in the owners.'

The doors at the back of the hall swung open. Hilton's mum and dad appeared. His mum waved and headed towards them. She shook hands first with Mr Morrison who was standing close by. 'I've heard a lot about you from Hilton,' she began. 'He speaks very highly of you and your wife. Oh, and your ferrets, of course.'

'With no Huxley in the running, we've all got a better chance,' Mrs Morrison said. 'Everything's up for grabs now.'

Hilton had a good feel about today.

Chapter Forty-Four – A New Mattress

The day flew over. The audience jumped to their feet as Hilton walked towards the head judge to collect his prize. Best National Junior Handler Award.

He felt as light as air, and his mum, dad, uncle and the Morrisons were cheering and whooping as he held the trophy above his head.

'A worthy winner. I'm sure you'll agree. And that concludes our championship programme for today. Safe journey home, folks.'

The applause continued as the results scrolled onto a big screen at the front of the arena.

WE ARE PLEASED TO CONFIRM THIS YEAR'S NATIONAL CHAMPIONSHIP WINNERS
WINNER -LONGEST TAIL – **BELLA**- OWNER, NORBERT NORRIS
WINNER -PINKEST NOSE- **JONTY**- OWNER, MORRIS MORRISON
WINNER -WIDEST YAWN- **JASPER**- OWNER, DORIS MORRISON
WINNER -AGILITY (HOB) -**OGDEN**- OWNER, NORBERT NORRIS
WINNER -AGILITY (JILL) – **WINIFRED**- OWNER, NORBERT NORRIS
WINNER -MAZE (HOB) -**JAGGER**- OWNER, NORBERT NORRIS
WINNER -MAZE (JILL) -**ELSA**- OWNER, NORBERT NORRIS
WINNER -FASTEST VETERAN – **HILDA**- OWNER NORBERT NORRIS
WINNER -BEST WORKING PAIR – **JACOB** AND **HANNAH**, OWNER NORBERT NORRIS
WINNER -GRAND NATIONAL (HOB)- **REUBEN**- OWNER NORBERT NORRIS
WINNER -GRAND NATIONAL (JILL)- **RUBINA**- OWNER NORBERT NORRIS

And the list went on.

'It's almost embarrassing,' Uncle Norbert said, as the family stood together watching the last of the large black letters travel up the screen.

BEST NATIONAL JUNIOR HANDLER- **HILTON HUGHES**

'It's a lifetime of your hard work, Uncle,' Hilton said, giving him a big hug.

'I couldn't have done it without you lad,' the old man replied, his eyes glistening as he pulled a big white hankie the size of a flag, from his trouser pocket. 'It's been quite a business, one way and another.'

'So, Huxley couldn't make it today?' Hilton's mum asked.

'He's tied up,' Mr Morrison smiled, '…on police business. Involved in stealing prize-winning ferrets from his competitors.' He winked at Hilton. 'And along with his reckless-driving trouble, it might be a while 'til we see him again.'

Everyone started to pack up their winners, feeding them grapes and the odd raw chicken wing. People were drifting out of the hall to head for home and the arena became quiet.

'Today's been the best. Hard to see how it could've been bettered,' the old man said, as he plopped down onto a chair. The arena doors swung open and a woman, older, wearing a short black coat, made her way inside. She was scanning around the room, trying to pick someone out.

Hilton noticed that beneath her black coat there was a long blue and white apron, with a big frill around the bottom. He was sure he'd seen something like it before. But, where?

His uncle took in a deep breath and stood up. 'I don't believe it….' he said. 'Izolda? Is that you?'

'There's such a lot to say, Norbert,' she started, 'but the first thing is… Congratulations! No one could be happier for you than me. You've always been a grafter. All you ever needed was that bit of luck.'

Hilton's mum and dad looked at one another, a little surprised.

'It was hard, going our separate ways,' she continued. 'I've been working in the Sales Department of Blaze's animal foods. But, I'm here today on their behalf, to offer a sponsorship deal to the winner. The face of your favourite ferret on their sacks of Blaze's Best, in return for a large cash sum.'

Uncle Norbert wobbled a little then sat down quickly. She went on, '…and maybe, we could talk about other things over a nice…'

'Cup of tea?' he said, his eyes fixed first on her smiling face, then wandering to take in the beautiful wad of money in her hand.

EVERYONE HELPED THE UNPACKING BACK at the East Northumbria Ferret Boarding and Welfare Society. As they returned the winners to the sheds, they put down bowls of chopped lettuce and banana for the lads and lasses left behind, as they finished up in Bluebell Lodge.

'It's a shame Mabel couldn't do The Maze today, but there'll be other times, won't there, Uncle? Hilton checked.

'Her work at home was too important,' Uncle Norbert explained, as together they peered into the jills' half of the pen and saw Mabel, a little wider than her previous ferret shape, accompanied by seven tiny kits snuggling close to their mother's body.

Norbert removed Rodders from his side of the cage and suspended him carefully, so he could see the babies, all healthy-looking, and each with one red eye and one brown.

'TIME TO GO HOME, Hilton,' his mum said. 'It's been a tiring day for you. Dad's put your equipment in the car.'

'My *equipment?*' he questioned.

'Uncle Norbert has something for you, to thank you for all the help,' she explained. 'Come and look.'

His dad popped open the boot and fitting snugly inside was a new hand-made wooden cage with a divider down the middle and a small ferret in each side. A water bottle was suspended on the wire front and a heavy bowl inside read, 'Blaze's Best'.

'But Mum and Dad, you don't like…' Hilton began.

'Uncle Norbert checked with Dad and me first,' his mum continued, 'but you can *still* come here of course, to help with the weas… stoa… ah… crikey… you know, the ferrets.'

'You've helped us in more ways than one, son,' his father went on. Other than keeping the promises he'd made about school Hilton had no idea what that could be.

'The National Championships is big business in the betting world.'

Hilton's heart fell to the floor. He'd forgotten about that. He had a bad feeling about what was coming next, but his dad was smiling.

'So, your mum and I agreed. I've wanted to give it up. Go out on top. One last bet on Norbert's ferrets today.' He patted his trouser pocket.

'And that means we're off on holiday at Christmas, the three of us. At last.'

'But what about Uncle Norbert?' Hilton asked.

'We've got something for you too, Norbert,' his dad went on, handing him a carrier bag from Phones2U. Norbert opened the box inside, and there was a little black mobile phone. Hilton's dad rang the number and it trilled out a special ring tone.

We're in the money,
We're in the money,
Let's spend it, lend it, send it, rollin' along.

'Seemed right for you, Norbert. Time you had a bit of modern technology.'

'I can change that for you, Uncle, if you prefer a different ringtone,' Hilton offered.

'I'm fine with that, lad.' The old man smiled as he glanced at the old blue and white apron now hanging up on the back of the kitchen door.

'I'll be sorted now,' he said. 'My new mattress is coming next Tuesday.'

Chapter Forty-Five – A Business of Ferrets

BY THE FOLLOWING SUMMER, PLANS for the new East Northumbria Ferret Boarding and Welfare Village were well underway.

A plumber worked with Hilton and Norbert to design self-rinsing and filling water troughs, while their joiner created pens which automatically tilted to allow soiled ferret bedding to slip away and be topped up from a container hidden in the ceiling. Izolda brought a feed specialist from Blaze's to design a dispenser providing the right amount of Blaze's Best, bought in sacks displaying Rodders' beautiful brown-eyed, red-eyed portrait. No more messy food bowls.

The pair, plus Rodders, often travelled to Bingley's to buy what they needed; locks, hammers and nails, and Hilton would always make sure they walked through the Christmas aisle.

Just in case.

IN THE WEEK BEFORE SCHOOL broke up for summer, when Hilton was planning to spend all his spare time preparing for this year's National Championships, Miss Sharkey promised he could do it.

Hilton's dad helped take everything he needed to school in the car.

'I know you've all been waiting for this,' she started, as the class stared in excitement at the ferret cage and the collection of furry cat snakes. Hilton's shoulders began to rise.

'Hilton, our resident ferret expert, agreed to bring some of his animals and talk to you about them. Since he fixed 'The Squirrel' last year,' she shot a look at Alanah who was smiling widely, 'we knew he was good with living things, and helping at his uncle's boarding and welfare society has made him even better. Let's have a round of applause for Hilton Hughes, please.'

It was like being at the National Championships again. Hilton got to his feet and swelled with pride.

'Are you happy to take questions, Hilton?' she asked.

'Can I tell a ferret joke first?' he asked.

His dad had made him practise, said it would help his nerves.

'When ferrets visit the theme park, which ride do they like best?' he asked, his fingers crossed behind his back, hoping no-one would know.

Everyone looked blank. They shrugged at one another.

'*The ferrets' wheel*!' he laughed, but he didn't need to worry. It got him off to a great start.

'What do they eat?' Imran asked.

'My mum says they smell. Is that true?' Brigid wanted to know.

'Are they part of the weasel family?'

There were many questions.

'Alanah, you have the last question?' Miss Sharkey said, as the end of day bell was about to sound.

'Yes,' she said, clearing her throat. 'I'd like to ask Hilton the secret of his success.'

Hilton thought. That's a tough one. Because the answer was a bit of a mystery. To him too. According to Uncle Norbert, Hilton was a lucky mascot.

And according to Hilton, it could have been one odd magical moment at Bingley's, or perhaps it was the Blaze's Best food. Or as his mum said, just being sensible and working hard.

'It's probably a combination of things,' he smiled. 'It was hard at first, but now I really enjoy having my own business of ferrets.'

As everyone was getting ready to leave for the day, Alanah shuffled up to Hilton in the corridor and whispered to him from the corner of her mouth.

'My dad came across an injured animal yesterday, but he doesn't know what to do with it. I've said you're his man.'

'Is it a squirrel?' Hilton asked.

Acknowledgements

A huge shout-out to the brilliant tuition and support of the staff on my recent MA in Creative Writing course at Newcastle University without whom this little story would never had emerged, but with particular thanks to Ann Coburn and Gabrielle Kent who kindly 'baptised' its first furry scuttle into the world.

Massive thanks go to my friends and fellow students on the MA course, especially Liz Haynes and Nicola Spain who read every word of many successive drafts and accompanied them with honest, positive feedback.

Helen Murthy, on her socially-distanced maternity leave from teaching secondary school English, took the time to provide me with great guidance on age suitability of the story, while Mrs Roseanne Galvin and her fabulous Year 6 class at Harlow Green Primary School read *A Business of Ferrets* aloud in class mid-pandemic, invited me to be interviewed by them for World Book Day, and made me feel like a 'proper writer'!

My lovely parents taught me from a very young age that nothing was ever out of bounds as long as you worked hard enough, so my daughters managed not to bat an eyelid when I decided to return to university 43 years after the very first time, and they behaved as if this was totally normal behaviour.

The patience and support of Rose Drew and Alan Gillott at Stairwell Books has been remarkable, unrelenting and much appreciated, along with the artistic talents of Sydney Luntz.

And finally, to the Beamish Open Air Museum where I first saw, at very close range, several wonderful ferrets in an exhibition provided by local aficionados. The owners were so proud of their work and their animals they'd had business cards printed, and only from politeness, I took one when it was offered. For the life of me, I couldn't imagine when I might have need of a ferret boarding and welfare society. I was however, transfixed by the little critters, handled one (with support) and consigned the business card to the zippy pocket of my Biba handbag. Months, possibly years later, that handbag was emptied and the card fell out onto my writing desk. The idea for A Business of Ferrets was born.

Other books for young people available from Stairwell Books

Shadow Cat Summer	Rebecca Smith
Very Bad Gnus	Suzanne Sheran
The Water Bailiff's Daughter	Yvonne Hendrie
Season of the Mammoth	Antony Wootten
The Grubby Feather Gang	Antony Wootten
Mouse Pirate	Dawn Treacher
Rosie and John's Magical Adventure	The Children of Ryedale District Primary Schools

For further information please contact rose@stairwellbooks.com

www.stairwellbooks.co.uk
@stairwellbooks

Lightning Source UK Ltd.
Milton Keynes UK
UKHW010709010921
389834UK00001B/26